BODY

AND

BLOOD

ALSO BY MICHAEL SCHIEFELBEIN

Vampire Vow

Vampire Thrall

Blood Brothers

Vampire Transgression

BODY

AND

BLOOD

Michael Schiefelbein

St. Martin's Minotaur

New York

This is a work of fiction. All of the characters, organizations, and events portrayed in this novel are either products of the author's imagination or are used fictitiously.

 For information, address St. Martin's Press, 175 Fifth Avenue, New York, N.Y. 10010.

www.minotaurbooks.com

Title page photo by Bruce Denney for openphoto.net cc: Attribution-ShareAlike

ISBN-13: 978-0-312-33019-4
ISBN-10: 0-312-33019-7

First Edition: September 2007

10 9 8 7 6 5 4 3 2 1

Dedicated to the Memory of

CLIFFORD EDMUND STRUNK

May 21, 1957–March 2, 1995

Part One

THE RETURN

Fear not, you shall not be put to shame;
you need not blush, for you shall not be disgraced.
The shame of your youth you shall forget,
the reproach of your widowhood no longer remember.

—ISAIAH 54:4

I

THE SCENE IN my head was vivid. I saw Jack Canston in a red tank top and black running shorts, kneeling with his sinewy arms outstretched, as if *he* were on the cross—not Jesus. He kept his eyes on the real crucifix, spotlighted above the holy tabernacle. I knelt next to him in the dark chapel, trying to keep my focus on the crucifix. Trying not to glance at Jack's shoulder muscles, like armor pauldrons on a medieval knight, trying not to watch Jack's Adam's apple move on his strong neck when he swallowed. When my outstretched arm brushed Jack's, my groin tingled.

"He's the crucified Lord," Jack whispered, "begging us to die with him." He squeezed his eyes shut in adoration, and tears trickled from his thick lashes, down his smooth cheeks. He was only sixteen and hadn't begun to shave. But hair grew thick in his armpits. I inhaled their sweaty odor. Before we had entered the dark chapel, I'd noticed that the back of Jack's red tank top was drenched with sweat. We had just finished a secret run on the country road winding around the seminary—while the other seminarians played pool or watched television in the recreation hall in the west building.

"The crucified Lord," Jack repeated. "Do you feel his love, Chris?"

"Yes." I glanced at the cross and then back at Jack. I wanted to kiss him and sink to the slate floor in his arms.

"He dies for us again," Jack continued. "Every day in mass. Every time the priest lifts the bread and says, 'This is my body, given up for you.'"

My body, given up for you. Given up for you. Given up for you.

THAT SCENE WITH Jack, a scene of long ago, faded, morphing into the scene before me now. The real Jack, an older Jack, stood before me. It had been twenty-five years since the scene in the dark sanctuary. Now the light of a waning winter afternoon settled in the airy chapel. And Jack, now forty-one years old, stood behind the altar, beautiful in a white chasuble. Thirty of us priests, also in white, crowded around him in the large, open space—like the heavenly host gathered around the Lamb in the Book of Revelation. All of us extended a hand toward the wafer as he lifted it and pronounced the words of consecration, his dark eyes raised to the soaring ceiling, "This is my body, given up for you." Jack's tone was softer now, all these years later, more reflective—marked by experience.

The years had left him even more handsome. His thin face had filled out, and his angular nose, jaw, and chin now made him look rugged rather than austere. Heavy stubble covered his cheeks, and his hair was thick and long and shabby—no longer combed back from his forehead and parted. His wiry body had thickened into a powerful mass of chest, shoulders, and arms. He exuded a rugged, faintly sleazy, sensuality.

Why had he returned, almost twenty-five years after breaking off contact with me and disappearing in the vastness of Montana? Why had he left his own diocese and his own family to return to the Archdiocese of Kansas City?

I couldn't stop staring at Jack through the rest of mass, with all of the old feelings rushing through me—feelings I thought had died long ago. Their intensity scared me. Jack scared me. When mass ended, I avoided him, removing my alb in the chapel and draping it over a pew rather than removing it in the sacristy where Jack and other priests went to disrobe.

Then I headed for cocktails in the library of what was now St. John's Diocesan Center. In the late eighties, after years of dwindling enrollment, the old high school seminary had been converted to administrative offices and a retreat center. I, now sixteen years a priest, was in charge of managing it, and I lived on the premises. The archbishop, who lived there as well, held a monthly gathering for his clergy—mass was followed by cocktails and dinner. Tonight, three days after Christmas, we celebrated the holiday.

I stood in line at the drink table, watching nervously for Jack's appearance. A crowd of priests mingled around a glowing Christmas tree in the center of the dimly lit room. The earnest faces of a few young guys stood out—boys still in love with the church they'd surrendered their lives to. But most of the priests were over fifty, paunchy, and dressed in nappy, stretched-out sweaters or faded clerical shirts with Roman collars.

As I poured myself a drink, Corey Mulhane fumbled toward the table. Corey's brown eyes were bloodshot. His full lips and pale, freckled cheeks hung loosely, as though his face was slipping off his skull. The boyish cuteness that lingered as he approached fifty seemed strangely grotesque whenever he drank.

"Nice little party, huh?" Corey said. "The archbishop loves his priests." He filled a glass with Scotch and raised it in a toast. "Here's to the church and its lovely twelve days of Christmas cheer."

I nodded doubtfully. Corey must have started drinking that afternoon before mass. He'd been off the wagon since his parents' death the year before—his mother's stroke coming just two months after his father's heart attack. But his parishioners at St. Michael's indulged their dimpled Irish darling, and the archbishop felt sorry for him, only gently nagging him to reenter the archdiocese's treatment program for parish priests.

We stepped over to a sitting area and settled on a leather sofa.

"How are you doing?" I said.

"Never better. Nice to be with the gang."

"How did Christmas masses go at St. Michael's?"

Corey smiled and snorted. "Fat Mary Conley belted out 'O Holy Night' again. The stroke didn't stop her, goddamnit. Year number fifteen."

I glanced at the door when someone entered. But it was only the archbishop, a bony man with a fringe of white hair. He wore a black jacket over his clerical shirt, and the pectoral cross he'd received on becoming a bishop was visible inside the lapels. We all applauded him.

"Thank you," the archbishop said, raising his hand as though offering an appreciative blessing. "You are good and faithful servants. After a busy Christmas in our parishes, I know you'd prefer to stay home on a cold night like this. Your sacrifice shows how fortunate I am as your shepherd. You truly inspire me!"

Corey was right. Archbishop Alfred Koch did love the priests of the three counties that made up the Archdiocese of Kansas City. And he bent over backward to keep them happy. He knew how overworked everybody was, a number of priests serving two or three parishes in rural areas. Little by little, lots of priests had abandoned their posts after the modernizing reforms of the Second Vatican Council in the 1960s awakened them to the beauty of the secular world. Most left to get married. More than a few found a place in the growing gay community—not that this was ever officially acknowledged. I'd learned more and more about the gay life in Kansas City through the Web site of the Gay and Lesbian Community Center. One of our ex-priests, a student I had admired back in high school, recently had become the center's president.

The church's return to staunch conservatism ushered in by John Paul II did attract some devout young candidates to the priestly ranks. Maybe their number would grow until the archdiocese returned to its smug days of glory, but if it did, the archbishop could say good-bye to some of the last liberal holdouts.

The archbishop's little speech triggered Corey's disgust with Roman hierarchy. He turned to me with a cynical expression and said, "Did you read what good old Cardinal Ramirez said in the Vatican rag?" He raised his chin and affected a snotty attitude as he quoted the cardinal: "Homosexuals are intrinsically disordered, incapable of spiritual leadership. Allowing homosexuals in the priesthood is 'absolutely inadvisable, imprudent, and risky.' "

"Jesus," I moaned. "Let the witch hunt begin."

Corey nodded. "Oh, it will. Of course, *you* have nothing to worry about. Father Seib is pure as the driven snow." Corey spoke with mock reverence. "Father Seib would give his chaste body over to be burned for the sake of Holy Mother Church."

"I don't think Ramirez is making any fine distinction between repressed homosexuals and active ones. He'd happily toss out anybody he suspected of ever having a wet dream about another man. Which would mean tossing out fifty percent of the clergy in every diocese—bishops included. Men who've given their lives to Holy Mother. Talk about ingratitude. And hypocrisy!"

Corey snorted. "You'll all just get more damned scared—and closeted."

"Whatever you say." I resisted getting drawn into the familiar argument. According to Corey, I'd sold out to the increasingly uptight church and turned into a pathetic, asexual zombie. Corey himself proudly joined gay organizations and went to an annual retreat for gay priests.

Corey looked ready to argue, but his attention suddenly shifted to the door. "Well, don't forget your virtue now that lover boy is finally here," he said. "I know you've been counting the minutes since his transfer was announced last month."

I turned, and there he was, accompanied by a pudgy old classmate, Reggie Lutz, jabbering in his ear. Jack looked tired, besieged, like this party was the last place he wanted to be.

"How nice," Corey quipped. "You two can reembark on the road to sainthood together—leave old sinners like me in the dust."

"He seems different," I said, oblivious to Corey's bantering. "Does he seem different to you?"

Corey sputtered a laugh.

"I mean besides being older. I know we're all older."

"But not wiser, apparently. You believe his story? Why he's back in the archdiocese?"

I shrugged off Corey's suspicions, whatever they were. "It *is* a lonely life in Montana. Jack told the archbishop that he had to drive three hours just to have lunch with another priest."

Corey smirked. "You think that's the reason—with all this crap going on around the country?"

"Oh, come on, Mulhane," I snapped. "Jack's not running from a sex scandal. And do you think if he was, the bishop would shield him? In today's climate? Jack wants a change. Don't we all deserve some kind of consolation after twenty years of this?"

"All right, don't get touchy. I'm sure the archbishop knows what he's doing."

In fact, I knew that the archbishop had investigated Jack before accepting him into the archdiocese. It wasn't unusual for priests to transfer from one jurisdiction to another for various reasons, but prudence demanded excellent references. The bishop of Montana apparently had no reservations about Jack.

"You haven't even talked to him yet, have you?" Corey said.

"I didn't get a chance," I lied. In truth, I'd put Jack in the apartment right next to mine, but I'd left him a note at the front desk instead of waiting to greet him in person. I didn't want our reunion to happen over luggage and practical questions about keys and thermostat problems. And I was afraid. Maybe I'd discover how deluded I'd been as a vulnerable teenager. Maybe my only experience of love had been a joke. Maybe Jack had never really loved me. After all, I was the one who had finally given in to my urges and gone to Jack's bed—the week before summer vacation our junior year. I was the one who had kissed him. He hadn't protested, and he had quickly taken charge in bed, but what did adolescent sex mean?

And even if it had meant something all those years ago, so what? We were kids then. This silly fantasy of mine sprang from a midlife crisis, from years of repression. But I was ripe for a fantasy. I was ripe for being swept off my feet and carried away into the sunset.

"Well, you two should be very cozy," Corey continued, covering his mouth to stifle a belch. "Canston and Seib, together again at the old stomping grounds. I can see you now, racing each other up the hill to the seminary. Kneeling side by side before the tabernacle in the wee hours. Ejaculating as you pass beneath doorways." Corey chuckled. "Wasn't that what you called it? *Ejaculating* little pious prayers to remind yourselves you were in the holy presence of God?"

"He's only here temporarily." My eyes were still on Jack. "Until they rebuild Santa Rosa's rectory." A fire had destroyed Santa Rosa's old mission-style parsonage just a week before Jack was due to arrive.

"Santa Rosa's still a Spanish-speaking parish," Corey said. "Where did Jack learn to speak the lingo? It sure as hell wasn't from old Rodriguez. Two years of classes and he never got us past *Hola, qué tal.*"

A picture of the jowly, bulbous-nosed Spanish teacher from our high school days popped into my head and made me smile. "Speak for yourself, Mulhane."

Corey dismissed me with a drunken wave, stood, and wobbled back to the bar.

I was on the verge of rescuing Jack from Reggie, when two more classmates approached him. So I gave up. I left the library and, through a connecting corridor to the main building, entered the chapel. The enormous, square space occupied most of the main building, which was in the center of the six-building complex. Wide corridors, like contemporary cloisters, surrounded the chapel on the lower level, while staff apartments, the library, and other common rooms surrounded it on the upper.

The white, roughly textured walls of the chapel rose to panels of clear, gable-shaped glass. The tentlike roof was intended to recall the Ark of the Covenant, which sheltered the tablets inscribed by God with the Ten Commandments. On bright days, light poured into the wide open space. Pews were arranged on three sides of a hefty altar of red granite sitting high on a slate platform. In the daylight, the chapel was clean and clear as a mountaintop retreat, the blue sky visible above snowy walls.

But the sun had long set when I entered the gallery. And at night, the sound of a cough or footstep echoed in the dark place like the cough or footstep of a lost child. Glowing in a spotlight, the golden corpus of Christ crucified hung on the towering reredos of granite that matched the altar.

The chapel had lost the magic of my high school days, when boyish camaraderie filled it. No matter how many retreats for old women I'd led here over the years, it would always rightfully belong to the ones who would never return: long-haired boys strumming guitars and banging tambourines at folk masses. It would always belong to me and Jack, freshly showered and smelling like soap after running ten miles in cross-country training, whispering together a litany of the Blessed Virgin, our elbows touching on the pew.

Sitting in the darkness now, the scent of candles lingering from mass, I felt numb instead of nostalgic. I felt tired and defeated and idiotic for hoping that Jack would come running after me. We were middle-aged priests who'd staffed a hell of a lot of parishes. We'd married scores of young couples, visited scores of sickbeds, and buried scores of the dead. We'd listened to every conceivable sin in the confessional, endured every conceivable parishioner complaint and parish faction. We'd sent straying husbands back to their families and even straying gay lovers back to their partners. Or at least, I had. Who knew how orthodox Jack had remained?

And with every gay couple I'd come across in parish ministry—and the numbers seemed to grow over the years—I resented my lonely, celibate life in a church increasingly hostile to those it considered disordered. I fantasized about sharing my life with another man—before it was too late.

Chatter in the corridor suddenly broke into my thoughts. It was dinnertime. I had no appetite and was in no mood to join the others in the dining hall. I decided to go up to my room. As I stood to leave, I heard someone behind me call my name.

It was Jack.

I turned and watched his shadowy form advancing. He genuflected before the tabernacle and came to the front pew where I sat.

"Corey said you were looking for me," he said, towering over me. "Why did you disappear?"

I shrugged, not knowing what to say.

"I need some fresh air," he said. "How about a walk?"

We got our coats and strolled out beyond the handball and tennis courts on the southwest side of the buildings. We made small talk along the way. Only an inch of snow lay on the ground, and the moon was high and bright. At the top of the hill at the western edge of the property, Jack lit a cigarette.

"When did you start smoking?" I was surprised that the self-disciplined Jack had succumbed to such a habit.

"A while back, during some parish crisis. I needed something to calm my nerves." Jack pulled up the collar of his pea coat. "We're on the old cross-country course. I remember this fence."

A split-rail fence demarcated the boundary between St. John's and a neighbor's farmland. Cows used to graze there as we sprinted by. But it had been years since the pasture held cattle.

The area around St. John's was mostly rural, with little towns like Bonner Springs and Basehor and Piper dotting the farmland. But downtown Kansas City was less than fifteen miles to the east, and the suburbs were gradually spreading and the city steadily incorporating more of Wyandotte County. Everyone knew that this idyllic setting was destined to vanish.

As we quietly walked along the old track, I pondered the idea of the steely Jack needing to calm his nerves. I'd always been the self-conscious worrier, and Jack had ordered me to renounce my perfectionism, as though someone could do that with a flick of a switch. As though Jack had ever needed to worry about perfection.

"The place looks different." He nodded toward the buildings. "With all the remodeling."

"I guess," I said. "I'm used to it now."

"I think it's a shame."

"It's a new world," I said. "Who wants to go back?" I meant go back to the days when I had stifled my feelings for Jack. But how could he know that? He didn't respond to my comment.

We talked about where we'd continued our seminary studies after St. John's. Jack was impressed that I'd gone to Rome for theology. He'd ended up at a conservative seminary in Indiana. After ordination, he'd volunteered to work in a mission in Monterrey, Mexico. That was where he learned Spanish. He said his time there was the happiest period of his life. He worked five years at the mission before returning to a parish back in Montana.

When we came to the two-lane road that led to the entrance of St. John's, we turned back, cutting across a field of unspoiled snow. The bell tower shone in the moonlight, a quarter of a mile away. The tower was formed by three slender white panels joined on top by arched crosspieces, creating an elongated, vaguely Gothic frame. The shape was repeated in the tall window moldings running in a continuous series around each of the seminary's six flat-roofed buildings, which were joined together by cloisterlike corridors. Along with the central building, the dorms on the south, and the dining and recreation building on the west, there were two large buildings on the north that housed the diocesan offices and an auditorium.

The simple, classic beauty of the place had won my heart the moment I set eyes on it at the age of thirteen, the child of a shabby, working-class neighborhood—unlike Jack's suburban professional clan.

"How is your family?" I said. "They still in Billings?"

"Fine," Jack said, quietly. "They're all just fine."

"They must hate to see you move away."

Jack lit another cigarette and blew a stream of smoke into the cold air. "It's God's will."

My heart sank. The old stern piety still possessed him.

We made our way up the long drive to the entrance. Inside the front doors, Jack asked me to say a rosary with him in the chapel.

"I don't think so," I said, pulling off my knit cap.

"Just one decade. Ten Hail Marys. For old time sake?" Jack grinned adorably.

I couldn't resist him. I followed him a short way down the front corridor and into the chapel. We knelt in a back pew. In his deep, grave voice Jack recited the first half of each Hail Mary and I chimed in with the rest. The rhythm of our voices brought back the old feeling of my oneness with him. But spiritual communion was no longer enough, if it ever had been.

When we'd finished, we sat quietly in the pew.

"Just like it used to be," he said.

"I thought you forgot."

"Never." Jack laid his hand on my thigh. "I want to show you something. Come up to my room."

Telling myself not to misinterpret his touch, not to hope, I followed him out of the chapel, up the front stairs by the entrance, and down the hallway that ran along the west side of the chapel. Like all the old faculty apartments, it consisted of a living room and a bedroom with a bath. In his living room, furnished with commercial-looking armchairs and a sofa, the floor-to-ceiling bookshelves held only two stacks of books and a few bottles of liquor. A canvas backpack and a full ashtray sat on the desk next to a glowing lamp. In the adjacent bedroom, a couple of bags sat on the floor by the bed, and some shirts hung in the open closet.

"Sit down," Jack said, dropping his coat on a green armchair. "You want a drink? I've got some Jack Daniel's. No ice, though."

Taking off my coat, I sat on the sofa and accepted the tumbler of bourbon.

Jack dug a thick manila envelope out of the backpack, dropped it in my lap, and sat next to me with his drink. "Go ahead," he said. "Open it."

When I dumped the contents on the glass coffee table, I immediately recognized my own handwriting on the folded notebook paper. "You kept my letters," I said, incredulous. I'd written to Jack for a whole year after he'd left St. John's. In the letters I'd told him I couldn't stand to be away from him. I couldn't stand not to hear from him. I apologized for making him sin that night. I said it was okay to love each other, wasn't it, if we stayed pure? I sent him prayers I'd composed just to show how pure I could be. I wanted him to say he loved me. But I might have settled for any word at all.

"I kept every one of them," he said.

"But you never answered them. You never returned my phone calls." Jack didn't come back to St. John's for senior year. In one of my attempts to reach him, his mother had answered the phone and told me he'd transferred to a high school in Montana.

"How could I? It was wrong. What we'd done. That's what I thought."

"So, it was just the sex? You'd committed a sin."

Jack shook his head. "It was being in love."

"Really?"

"Can you blame me? Take a look." Jack pulled a photo from the pile of letters. It was a picture of me at seventeen, stepping into red sweatpants after a cross-country race on the St. John's course. Broad-shouldered, skinny, and long-haired, I was smiling my usual crooked smile at the camera. "You looked like a young Brad Pitt."

"You think so?" Flattered, I took a swig of bourbon.

Jack nodded emphatically. He tossed back his own drink and refilled our glasses. His evening beard was heavy. I wanted to stroke it.

"Have I changed a lot?" I ventured. "Aside from gaining thirty pounds and a wrinkle or two."

Jack smiled and ran his fingers through my now short hair. "You're still beautiful."

"I still love you," I suddenly blurted. "I know it's crazy. But here we are at St. John's again. It's like you never left."

"That's how I feel. That's how I knew I'd feel coming back." He leaned over and pecked me on the lips. Then he kissed me deeply.

I wanted him to swallow me. Or maybe I wanted to swallow him.

"Can we go to your room?" he whispered. "My bed's covered with boxes."

Groggy and excited all at once, I led him next door to my apartment.

LOOKING BACK NOW at our first night in bed, I realize that I should have known something was wrong. Something beyond Jack's eventual explanations. The way he wrestled me to the mattress, shoved my body this way and that, forced me on my stomach and rammed himself into me—barely waiting for me to hand him the lube that I kept in the nightstand for my own needs. And then the moaning after he was spent—like a wounded animal—and the tears I felt on my neck.

Maybe I should have suspected something, but I was already caught up in a dream that seemed too good to be true. Nothing about it seemed possible. So I wasn't in a position to separate what made sense and what didn't.

Besides, I was sixteen again. And I knew nothing of sexual relationships, let alone strange sex. I'd had guilty fantasies over the years, but I'd kept my celibacy vow, partly by telling myself I wasn't deprived. After all, I'd told myself, I had experienced love—albeit in one fleeting moment.

And on the night of our reunion, I *wanted* to read his roughhousing as a sign of his passion for me. As it was—at least in part.

2

WHEN THE WINTER dawn filtered through the bedroom blinds the next morning, I was already awake and staring at Jack. He lay on his side facing me, his muscular arm outside the bulky teal comforter, his head resting on his other arm, his long hair in his eyes. We'd been up until four. Still deep in the first sleep cycle, he breathed through his mouth.

He reeked of nicotine. I usually hated the smell. But on him, it was alluring. Maybe it was a symbol of his new wildness and sensuality.

As a priest, I knew I should have felt guilty. But, instead, I felt triumphant as I watched him sleep, his faced shadowed in a heavy beard. I'd had the unconquerable Jack—and vindicated my own stifled longings.

I lay back to bask in the glory, reaching for his hand and pressing it against my chest. On the dresser, I could make out my crumpled shirt next to a Roman collar. Jack had peeled it off me and tossed it there before he kissed the back of my neck. As his lips had traveled across my shoulders, I'd stared gratefully at the crucifix above the dresser, a piece of Latin American folk art. The painted Jesus was brown and smiling amid bright red birds and yellow flowers.

It was after seven, and I had a nine o'clock appointment to prepare for—a diocesan accountant wanted to go over business records. I gently released Jack's hand, climbed out of bed, and went into the bathroom to brush my teeth.

As I stood before the mirror, I had a new appreciation for my broad, sloping shoulders, square jaw, and shy green eyes. Jack had lusted after this man in the mirror.

The alarm clock buzzed in the bedroom. A moment later, the bathroom door opened and Jack appeared behind me in the mirror.

He mumbled a "good morning" on his way to the toilet. As he relieved himself, he stared straight ahead at a blue and yellow Mexican blanket from Cozumel hanging on the wall. Was he avoiding my eyes? Did he regret last night?

"You sleep all right?" I said, to test his mood.

He nodded, still not glancing at me.

Now I panicked. "What's wrong? Are you sorry about last night?"

He gave me a look of complete surprise. "Why should I be sorry?"

"You looked grumpy."

"You wore me out." He nodded to his dick, which he was shaking now.

I approached him and pressed myself against his bare back, caressing his chest. As I clung to him, I rejoiced that this solid, hairy man was not the cold, scrawny boy I had known. He was grown up, free to do what he wanted. And we were lovers! I imagined that the bathroom was in our own house and we were getting ready for work. Maybe there was a little cocker spaniel on our bed. And a newspaper waiting for us in the front yard. We had never been priests, cold and chaste, behind the church's iron bars.

Jack would whisk me away to a world I'd been longing for, more and more intensely as I approached forty, afraid I'd miss out on life because of a church that condemned my nature.

Jack kissed my hand and left the bathroom. When I emerged, he was dressed in the clothes he'd removed the night before, even though there was no need to take the trouble. He could have walked naked down the hallway to the very next door to put on fresh clothes. I thought he might have worried about running into the archbishop, as unlikely as that was since the archbishop's apartment was at the front of the building.

I followed him into my living room.

The room was bright now, and Jack looked around admiringly at the teak furniture and big Navajo rug on the floor, at the books neatly arranged on the shelves behind my uncluttered desk.

"You haven't changed a bit," he said, turning to me. His eyes were puffy and bloodshot. "Organized to a T."

"That's not what you used to say." I adjusted the blinds because the rising sun was shining in my eyes. "You used to call me compulsive. Remember? 'You've gotta renounce this urge to control, Chris. Only God is in control.'"

Jack nodded sadly, as though he wished he could live by that advice now. I wondered why, but he was eager to get to Santa Rosa's, so I didn't pursue it. I told him I'd have dinner ready in the little staff dining room when he got home. For him and the archbishop, who wanted to eat with us. As he moved to the door, I waited, praying that he would turn around and kiss me without prompting. He did, a little awkwardly, not used to romantic good-bye rituals.

"I'm glad I found you again," he whispered.

"Me, too."

AS I WORKED that day, he was on my mind. I kept saying things to myself—words like mental pinches to make sure I wasn't dreaming: *I have a lover. I'm not alone anymore. To hell with the priesthood.* It was great to be sixteen again.

I frequently glanced at photos on my office wall, of families from parishes I'd served—couples I'd married, their new babies, graduation pictures of their teenagers. And my fantasy from the morning in the bathroom revived. Jack and I could be a couple. We could be our own family, invite friends to backyard cookouts. I imagined the children of my former parishioners playing tag and taking turns on a tire swing suspended from an oak.

At five, I told my secretary I was leaving for the day, locked my office door, and went to my apartment. I removed my clerical shirt and black trousers and retrieved a pair of faded jeans and a sweatshirt hanging on a hook in my closet. While I dressed I gazed fondly on the teal comforter that had wrapped Jack and me like a sun-warmed sea.

I headed to the west building to make dinner, strolling cheerily past the chapel and into the connecting corridor that ended in two sets of stairs, one going up to the kitchen and dining facilities and the other down to the pool and gym. I climbed the stairs and entered the large dining room where the seminarians used to eat in the old days and where now retreatants and conferees dined. It was an inviting, unpretentious hall with huge expanse of creamy linoleum tiles. The hall held fifty round tables covered in walnut Formica, with padded chrome chairs upholstered in orange vinyl. During the day-time, the warm light of the sun streamed through the hall's skylights and floor-to-ceiling windows. Now the hall only glowed garishly under the fluorescent lights I'd flicked on.

Behind the west wall of the dining room was a large industrial kitchen, and to the left of that were a smaller kitchen and dining room once used by the priests who had staffed the seminary. Only the archbishop and I used the staff areas now. I wound through the tables and entered the staff dining room where paneled walls glowed softly in the light cast by a tall lamp on the buffet.

In the little kitchen, I found a box of angel hair pasta and a jar of marinara sauce in the cupboard. For tonight, with the archbishop intruding, these would do. I cooked some sausage and added it to the sauce with plenty of fennel. And I threw a spinach salad together and heated a loaf of French bread I found in the freezer. I set the table in the dining room, digging up some cloth napkins and even a basket of dried flowers for the centerpiece.

Jack showed up at six-thirty, still in his short-sleeved black clerical shirt but with the white collar tab stuck in his breast pocket. He looked tired.

"Something smells good," he said.

I set down the pitcher of water I was using to fill the glasses and kissed him.

He grabbed my shoulders. There was an odd helplessness in his eyes. "I've been thinking of you all day." He kissed me.

"Is everything all right?" I said.

Before he could answer, the door opened, and he drew away from me.

The archbishop entered the room in his black jacket and trousers, crisp and wrinkle-free as ever, but he looked tired and troubled. I was afraid that he suspected something, and I watched him nervously as he poured us all a glass of the Scotch he kept in the buffet.

"I have some bad news," he said. "Edward Gerhardt is dead."

"Eddie?" I thought I'd misheard. Eddie Gerhardt, an old classmate from St. John's, was now the pastor of a church in Topeka. He hadn't attended last night's gathering, but neither had a lot of priests. "I just saw him last week. He was fine. We went to movie." I glanced at Jack, who looked as shocked as I was.

"He committed suicide," the archbishop said gravely, his gaze dropping to his glass. "His housekeeper found him this morning in the garage. In his car. He'd started it with the garage door closed. He was there all night."

Eddie's car was a vintage 1949 Plymouth. He liked to wear a tweed golf cap and big bow tie when he drove it. The getup made him feel like he was in an old movie, and he loved old movies. The week before, we'd taken the Plymouth to see *The Sound of Music,* the kickoff film of a retro festival.

"I can't believe it," I said. "Why? Did he leave a note?"

"Yes." The archbishop pursed his lips disapprovingly. "But I don't want to discuss it."

Now I knew. Eddie had confessed his secret sin, the one he shared with me—as he liked to put it. "We're abominations," he would say morosely, using the church's word for unnatural creatures like us. Then he would wait for my reassurance that the church was wrong. I had tried to reassure him, often. God made us the way we are, I'd tell him. We're not evil. But my reassurances never seemed to convince him. He had never stopped praying to be cured of his disorder. His self-loathing had finally come to this. He'd killed himself. But why only now? Why suddenly now?

Stunned, Jack and I listened as the archbishop reminded us that a priest's suicide was sure to scandalize our people. "They know that taking one's life is a mortal sin. It's bred of absolute despair of God's grace. For a priest to do this, for whatever reason, is unthinkable." The archbishop shook his head for shame. "For this reason, it's even more profane. Undoubtedly, people in the archdiocese will speculate over Edward's motives. But it's our duty to discourage such a fruitless exercise. We could simply suggest that Father Gerhardt was going through a bout of depression—which he surely was. We have to reassure the faithful that he undoubtedly repented in his final moment of consciousness—that our hope for such repentance warrants a Christian burial."

When we sat down to eat, the archbishop at the head of the table, he prayed for Eddie's soul and Eddie's family. Then he told us he'd just returned from a visit with Eddie's mother in Wamego, almost a two-hour drive away. "Of course, she's still in shock," he said, spooning sauce on his spaghetti.

"I can't imagine what she's going through," I said. I felt sorry for her, even though I had never liked her or the rest of Eddie's family. The Gerhardts were mean-spirited and vengeful. Eddie had inherited the traits. His charm and sense of humor could quickly give away to spite.

"She must be going through hell." Across the table from me, Jack broke off a piece of French bread from the loaf. He'd had two drinks, and he was a little blurry eyed. "A priest is a symbol. He's Christ among the people. To kill himself—I can't imagine anything more shameful for a family."

He continued along this line, the archbishop's head bobbing in agreement. Then the archbishop launched into a diatribe about the priest's symbolic role and how Eddie had betrayed such a sacred trust.

Finally, I couldn't take it anymore. I slammed down my fork. "Maybe he is a symbol," I blurted, "the symbol of a church that treats its members like children who can't think for themselves."

I spouted off several more grievances against the church, omitting the one I really believed to be responsible for Eddie's death—the teaching that branded him as a pervert. I could have gone on, but Jack was looking furious, and the archbishop, browbeaten. And I knew the liquor was talking and we were all upset about Eddie's suicide. And what I really wanted was to climb into bed with Jack and hold him all night. So I stopped myself.

"I'm sorry," I said to both of them. "But Eddie's not a symbol to me. He's my friend. We just went to see *The Sound of Music.* You know what he did at the theater? He farted like a trumpet, and then he glared at the woman two seats over like she was to blame—so everyone behind us could see him. That's Eddie. He's a jokester. A performer." By now it was finally sinking in that Eddie had killed himself. "And I love him." I barely got the words out, I was so choked up.

"It's all right, Chris," the archbishop said, touching my wrist. "We've all had a shock."

I looked at Jack for reassurance, but his eyes were lowered and he seemed lost in thought.

We finished the gloomy meal with little conversation. After we washed the dishes, the archbishop suggested going to the chapel to pray for Eddie. I didn't want to. The archbishop didn't know Eddie as I knew him. I didn't want to pray using the archbishop's words. And I didn't want to share my grief with someone who was judging Eddie.

But I felt I had no choice. The three of us went to the dark chapel and knelt in a pew near the tabernacle, the archbishop between Jack and me—as though he were our chaperon. I suddenly wanted to break loose from the man's hold on our lives. I didn't want to be at his mercy, as Eddie had been. As we prayed the rosary for the repose of Eddie's soul, I recited the responses like an automaton, just wanting to get them over with so I could absorb the horror of Eddie's death by myself. So I could replay conversations with Eddie in my mind, looking for clues that he was considering suicide.

Finally, we finished the rosary. The archbishop asked us to leave him alone in the chapel. We left quietly and didn't talk all the way up to our rooms. I thought Jack was mad. But when we came to his door, he took me in his arms. We went on to my apartment.

WHEN I WOKE up the next morning, Jack was propped on his elbow, staring at me in the pale light.

"How long have you been awake?" I mumbled, worried that my breath was bad.

"A while," Jack said, tickling my chest.

"Are you pissed about what I said last night? About the church?"

He smiled and shook his head. "You were upset."

"But I meant it."

He looked unconvinced. "You've given your life to the church."

"Tell me about it. Maybe it's time to move on." I paused and ventured, "Maybe God brought us together for a reason."

He studied me as though I'd said something curious. "I would never leave the priesthood," he said.

The panic I suddenly felt was like a vise crushing my chest. The pressure seemed to force blood into my head. It felt ready to explode. For a moment I couldn't speak. Finally, I choked out the words, "What about us?"

He smiled and patted me on the chest. Then he got up and dug his cigarettes from the breast pocket of his clerical shirt, which lay on an armchair in the corner. He lit one and sat in the chair, his bare legs spread, his hands clasped on his hairy chest.

"We can be together, just the way we are," he said confidently.

"It doesn't bother your conscience to break the vow of celibacy?"

"It's not a vow. It's a promise. Only priests in religious orders take vows."

I sat up in the bed and leaned against the headboard. "That's just a technicality."

"Not the way I see it. It was a promise created for practical reasons." He went on to explain what I already knew: diocesan priests were allowed to marry until the Middle Ages. The church had finally put a stop to it because church property was being inherited by the wives and children of priests. "So celibacy is just a practical discipline. There's a hierarchy of church doctrine. You know that. Celibacy is low on the list. And disobeying it is a lesser evil. Better to stay a priest and take a lover than abandon the flock."

The man uttering this sophistry sounded just like the Jack I had known in high school. So rational and cocksure. All the neediness I'd seen in his eyes the night before had vanished. He sat complacently smoking like king of the world. His arrogance was seductive—as it had been in the olden days. I slipped into my old way of thinking. *Jack knows best. Let him do the thinking.* Maybe I could have it both ways: safe in the priesthood and safe in Jack's arms.

I got up and went to him, dropping to my knees, taking his dick into my mouth. He sat back and let me.

A thought occurred to me, and I drew back. "How many lovers have you had?" I said.

"Does it matter? I've never been in love with anyone else."

"I want to know." I got up and sat on the bed, waiting.

Jack shrugged. "I don't know. I've gone to bed with a dozen or so over the years."

"Where did you meet them? In your parishes?"

"No. In bars. It was just sex."

"You didn't feel guilty?"

He gave me a haughty look, as though such a childish idea had never entered his head. "I kept it separate. What happened in the dark had nothing to do with the daylight."

I didn't like this answer, but apparently in that moment my fantasy about Jack and me was stronger than my reason. I dropped to my knees again in front of him. He guided my mouth back to his dick and in the ecstasy of tasting him, I gave up worrying about my competition.

OVER THE NEXT few days, Jack and I established a routine. We got up at seven, he left for Santa Rosa's by eight, and I was behind the desk in my office by eight-thirty. We connected by phone at least once during the day, sometimes two or three times. When he returned at six, we'd have a drink in my living room. Then we'd either head to the dining room for the dinner I'd prepared just for us—the archbishop was out of town—or we'd go out to eat.

No conferences or retreats were booked at St. John's the week Jack arrived, so I was free in the evenings. I helped him unpack his things and put them away. Most of his boxes were filled with books—mostly biographies of the saints and theology volumes, including an eight-volume set of Thomas Aquinas's *Summa Theologica*. One box was full of CDs, mostly redubbings of classic rock groups—Yes, Kansas, the Who, the Eagles.

The only things he'd brought to hang on the walls were a crucifix and two icons of the Virgin Mary—not a single photograph. When I asked him about it, he reminded me of the importance of spiritual detachment. No warm and fuzzy links to home allowed. No souvenirs from the Grand Canyon or the Royal Gorge, where he'd traveled with his family. No favorite blankets.

The familiar austerity scared me. Maybe I would end up being sacrificed, too, for the sake of religious perfection. Then I thought maybe passion would win him over. When I came across a box of pine figures he'd lovingly carved—an elk, a giraffe, and a sailboat—I thought I had a reason to hope.

Once he was unpacked, we spent little time in his drab apartment. In the evenings, we walked across the fields or swam laps in the Olympic-size pool in the west building. Then we watched TV or a video in my apartment, before Jack disappeared into the chapel for an hour of prayer. When he emerged, he looked bedraggled, like he'd wrestled with Satan. Once he looked like he'd been crying. When I asked him about it, he shrugged it off, said that he'd been moved by deep communion with Christ.

In some ways, it was like old times back at St. John's. Only better. No study hall. No mandatory night prayer. No obnoxious classmates to share Jack with. Just the two of us together, with the run of the place, like kids with vacationing parents, the whole house to themselves.

Of course, my thoughts often turned to Eddie, those first days after his death. The pimply, smirking face of his teen years popped up in the chapel and the corridors. I even saw his skinny body skipping like a girl out of the old dormitory. But Eddie's adolescent effeminacy had always disgusted Jack, and I didn't want to subject Eddie or his suicide to Jack's scrutiny. So I kept my sad thoughts to myself.

Every night we crawled into my bed and devoured each other in passion. I wanted him in me, and he knew it. So he teased me to excitement and made me beg for him. My mouth traveled over every inch of him, the high arches of his feet, the mounds of his calves, his furry belly and chest. Every night my climax electrified every nerve in my body. His made him moan like a wounded animal.

What was the pain deep inside him? One night, while I stroked his belly, I asked him. He smiled mysteriously and said, "Death."

"Death?" I was a little creeped out, my thoughts going to Eddie again.

"Ecstasy's like death. St. John of the Cross said so. Merging with the Other. Leaving our body behind."

"Whatever," I said. "As long as you don't really die inside of me."

He picked up my hand and kissed it. "That wouldn't be so bad."

I frowned and jerked my hand away at the morbid suggestion.

Jack Canston's Journal

December 31

Gotta keep it all separate—spirit and flesh, heaven and earth, all the rest. Let God take care of God's business and me take care of mine. Otherwise I'll end up back in the fucking nightmare of disinfectant, the walls closing in on me.

The ride from Montana helped me breathe. Drove with the window down from Sheridan to Cheyenne with the freezing cold in my face. Spotted twelve elk along the road. God's beautiful creatures.

No more Montana. Said good-bye to the family. The old man preached his usual number. Big and white-headed and braying like an ass. Inside the walls, I listened to him like a zombie. Clear-headed, I wanted to kick his sorry ass. Seventy years old or not. What does he know about it? The last thing I need is fucking judgment. Well, he loves God. So, his weakness is like the flesh. All grass. I shouldn't give a shit. It's all behind me.

Santa Rosa's is right for me. Parishioners are like the Mexicans in Monterrey. Those were great years in Monterrey. Everything stayed clean and divided. God's perfect church and us humans going about our business.

St. John's is the same. Home away from home. But I miss the guys from those days—Gomez and Deghand and Colombe especially—great runners. It was a lot of fun fucking around with Gomez on guitars. The place feels empty without all the rest, and no longer spanking new.

Seib's the same and different. Back then, he was beautiful, but he was the disciple. Now, he's still beautiful but he's got a fucking strong will of his own. In fact, he's got . . . I don't know what it is. Whatever it is, I need it. At least until the nightmares stop.

It's better not to think it all through. It's like Eddie, past and present, killing himself in a garage. Everyone knows he lived a tortured life.

But better not to think about Eddie, Canston! Better to love the Holy Catholic Church and do as you will.

3

EDDIE'S FUNERAL DIDN'T take place until the Saturday after his death, a whole week later. The delay allowed more of his parishioners to attend and some of his mother's people who were stuck in an Ohio snowstorm.

The day before, a foot of snow fell on us, too. It sat like thick icing on the black branches around the buildings. In every direction, a silent ocean of white stretched to the horizon, etched here and there with dark trees. The old handball court on the west side of the buildings rose from it like a giant gray iceberg. Beyond it, on the hill that sloped up to the adjoining farmland, the split-rail fence traced a brown line across the white, and the walls of a barn made a rusty smudge.

The overcast sky was like another fluffy sea. Muffled from below and above, the air was soundless. And as cold as a witch's tit, as Eddie used to say, relishing his stock of old-fashioned expressions.

Eddie's wake had taken place the day before, during the snowstorm. Jack and I hadn't braved the weather to attend. But on the day of the funeral, traffic reports claimed that I-70 was passable now. Still, in case there were delays, we left two hours before the funeral. The rural road to the east of St. John's hadn't been cleared, but Jack's pickup plowed through it easily. We turned onto Highway 24, which led south to the I-70 turnpike, connecting Kansas City to the east with Lawrence and Topeka to the west.

Plows had cleared the turnpike, and the light traffic heading west, away from Kansas City, rolled steadily along. Snow on the hilly land around the road undulated across the fields and drifted against trees and fences. Next to Jack, who sat at the wheel in a puffy black jacket, smelling of aftershave lotion, I felt snug and safe amid the cold, white expanse.

In twenty minutes, we passed Lawrence, which was growing into a trendy college town with new housing developments stretching to the interstate. And in another twenty minutes, we spotted the capitol dome of Topeka in the distance. We took the exit on the northeast side of town, cut through white farmlands, and drove across the straight five miles of Seward Avenue, where the Shawnee Indians used to race through what eventually became my old neighborhood of Oakland. German and Mexican immigrants had built wood frame houses there around the Santa Fe railroad shops.

As we climbed Branner Bridge, which spanned the sprawling railroad yard, the modest city skyline rose before us—a handful of tall buildings, a water tower, and the missile-shaped dome of the capitol building.

On the other side of the bridge we passed warehouses and grain elevators along the Kansas River, finally arriving at St. Mary's, a red brick church with twin steeples, built by German settlers. The parking lot across the street was full, and cars were crowded along the curb in front of the church. Jack parked up the block. We slipped on our knit caps and crunched through the snow back to the church.

Inside, people lined up in the narthex to view Eddie's body for the last time. The coffin of solid oak sat at one end of the narrow hall, between tall candle-stands and beneath an age-darkened painting of the Madonna.

A sense of dread weighed on me. I had presided over hundreds of funerals as a priest, but this dead man was my friend. And I was afraid that his final despair might have fixed on his face the look of self-loathing that he usually kept hidden behind a charming smile.

As we waited in line to pay our respects, a short, stocky woman in a black mantilla approached Jack. She was accompanied by a beautiful boy in a bomber jacket. He must have been in his early twenties. Jack introduced them to me as Mrs. Flores and her son Danny, parishioners from Santa Rosa's.

"Oh, Father," Mrs. Flores said, teary-eyed, "Father Edward looks so peaceful. It's hard to believe he's gone." If she knew how Eddie had died, she kept the shameful knowledge to herself. She rattled on about the good showing of Santa Rosa's parishioners and about how Eddie, on top of his full-time responsibilities at St. Mary's, had served so devoutly as a part-time minister at their church before Jack arrived.

While she spoke, Danny stared admiringly at Jack. And I stared at Danny. I was stunned by his Latin good looks, the swarthy, classical symmetry of his features. His lips were full, his strong neck perfectly sculpted, and his eyes as dark and bright as black onyx. On first glance, they seemed to emit a charming innocence, but quickly they revealed something else, the kind of willed deference that you find in the gaze of a new marine who's learned to discipline his rebellious spirit.

While Danny spoke to Jack about some book on spirituality, Mrs. Flores chatted with me. When she discovered I'd grown up in Oakland, she smiled and squeezed my hand, taking to me like the proverbial fish to water. She began pouring out her heart about the struggles of being a good parishioner while running a restaurant. Danny finally guided her into the church.

Jack and I stood in line for another five minutes. When only one person stood between us and the coffin—a hunched old man—I glimpsed Eddie's white and gold chasuble, and my heart raced. The man made the sign of the cross and stepped aside.

There lay Eddie before our eyes. Both of the casket's lids were raised, exposing the whole length of his long body. In a white and gold chasuble and black patent-leather shoes, Eddie looked like a life-size doll, all dressed up and painted. He reminded me of the Infant of Prague—the robed and crowned figurine of the Christ child under a glass dome that you see everywhere in churches built by Eastern Europeans. Eddie himself was devoted to the Infant. His own cherished glass-encased statue stood on a lace doily in his study.

At first I gazed at him as if he were just a waxwork curiosity. But when the first impression passed and I realized that this really was Eddie—with his still-boyish face, pug nose, and perfectly parted hair, now completely gray—my eyes filled up. I thought of his charming quaintness, his genuine devotion to God and to the church. Devotion as genuine as Jack's. I felt ashamed of my cynicism and of my temptation to chuck the priesthood.

Eddie's hands, entwined with a black rosary, were folded on his chest. The nails on his long, tapered fingers needed trimming, and I felt annoyed at the undertakers for neglecting them. Then I noticed that Eddie's rosary ring was missing from his right index finger. He'd bought it on our trip to Lourdes fifteen years before. He'd bathed in the miraculous waters from the spring that marked the spot where the Virgin Mary had appeared to little Bernadette Soubirous. He liked to turn the ring with his thumb, praying on its ten turquoise beads while he drove the Plymouth. I'd never seen him without it.

I turned to Jack and whispered, "Where's his rosary ring from Lourdes? He never took it off."

Jack had been gazing solemnly, almost fearfully, at Eddie's body, as though it confirmed the evil that humans were capable of. Now he glanced at Eddie's hand and threw me a look of concern without uttering a word.

"Maybe his mother wanted to keep it," I said.

He nodded, looking reassured that the sacred token was accounted for. Then he made the sign of the cross over Eddie, and we passed through the crowd and into the church, which was already half-filled with people bundled in coats. We traveled down the long center aisle toward the looming oak reredos. In its large central niche was a painted trio of statues. On either side of a pale Christ on a cross stood the Virgin Mary and Saint John, their hands devoutly clasped on their breasts. Painted on the ceiling of the apse, high above the reredos, another crucified Christ stretched out his arms. A wizened, bearded God hovered behind the cross, his robes flowing as though he and Christ were both weirdly sailing across the sky. Eddie had loved this strange duplication of crosses, as though a church could never have too much of a good thing.

Genuflecting together before the tabernacle at the base of the reredos, Jack and I entered the sacristy door in the apse.

In the long room, the archbishop and a dozen priests were already donning their albs and stoles. The archbishop looked haggard. In his white chasuble he stood at the window, clearly wishing to be left alone. The priests were subdued, moving into their best automatic, dutiful mode. It was in preparation for a ritual, even one marking a horrible tragedy, that they shone as examples of faith and composure. I felt proud that Jack and I belonged to such a brotherhood.

Jack and I added our coats to a pile on a table. We put on our albs and waited silently as more priests entered the crowded sacristy.

When the bell finally tolled, the twenty-five of us filed out the back door of the sacristy and around to the vestibule where the casket, now draped in a white pall, waited. Six of Eddie's nephews rolled it on its bier into the rear of the church, a large open area. The archbishop performed the initial rite. The organ introduced a hymn, and the priests marched in pairs down the long aisle to front pews reserved for them, passing beneath the drawn swords of the Knights of Columbus, in red capes and hats with plumes. Eddie would have loved the pageantry.

In assisting the archbishop, I took my place on the sanctuary dais, facing the congregation. Even the choir loft was full. I spotted young Danny and his mother there.

Eddie's four brothers and three sisters stood stern-faced and dry-eyed in the front rows near the casket. A white-headed Mrs. Gerhardt dabbed her eyes but kept her stoic gaze on the tabernacle. They all saw themselves as superior, socially and religiously—at least, they had during Eddie's high school days, the last time I had set foot in the Gerhardts' home. In their little German parish, their soybean acres and their expensive clothes gave them clout and a sense of entitlement.

The archbishop's eulogy was masterful, dodging any hint of shame associated with Eddie's death. He praised Eddie's dedication as a priest and raised his hands to draw attention to the renovations that Eddie had supervised as pastor of St. Mary's: repaired stained-glass windows and a refurbished organ in the loft. The archbishop committed Eddie's soul to the angels and reassured Eddie's family that Father Edward Gerhardt was preparing a place for them in heaven.

AFTER THE FUNERAL, the motorcade took twenty long minutes to reach the cemetery. In the bitter cold, on a hill reserved for the graves of priests, the archbishop led the prayers of internment under an awning that shuddered in the wind. I handed him the sprinkler filled with holy water. While the members of Eddie's family blessed the casket with it, I spooned incense on the coal I'd lit for the final veneration of the body. Smoke swirled up around the bare metal as though it were carrying Eddie's body to God.

I searched the huddled crowd for Jack's face and spotted it among the priests, the collar of his pea jacket up, a ski cap on his head, his eyes closed in prayer. Danny stood by him, his beautiful head bowed.

By the time the graveside service was over, big flakes of snow were sifting through the clouds, and the wind whipped coats and scarves as the crowd trudged back to their cars.

I briefly offered my condolences to Mrs. Gerhardt and was moving to join Jack when Miguel Diaz, an old classmate, approached me. A furry, Cossack-looking cap covered most of his blue-black hair. The padding of his dark wool coat made his wide shoulders seem enormous.

I hugged him and asked him what he was doing back from Rome. He was on staff at the American seminary there.

He smiled with embarrassment, lowering his beautiful chestnut eyes. "I've been appointed the auxiliary bishop of Santa Fe. I'm in the States to make arrangements for the move."

"Congratulations!" I patted his arm.

"I flew up from Santa Fe when I heard about Eddie. God forgive him." Miguel made the sign of the cross.

"God forgive us all," I said, "for not giving Eddie what he needed."

Miguel nodded humbly, but then added in a low voice, "I've heard horrible rumors about him."

"What do you mean?"

Miguel glanced around before answering. "That he was involved in a homosexual relationship."

This was news to me. "Who said that?"

Miguel shook his head as though he was not allowed to break a confidence.

"I don't believe it. Eddie and I were friends. I'd know if he was involved with someone." Only my sense of loyalty made me say this. The truth was, I probably wouldn't have known. Eddie's shame would have made him keep his mouth shut—except in confession.

"I only pray that Eddie wasn't involved in something like that," Miguel said sanctimoniously. "If he died with such a sin on his soul . . ." He evidently couldn't bring himself to finish this horrible thought.

I had almost suggested that Miguel and I go have lunch. After his remark, I was glad I hadn't. I wanted to get as far away from him as I could. I glanced across the cemetery and saw Jack talking to Danny near an enormous stone angel. Mrs. Flores was nowhere in sight. A sudden rush of jealousy prompted me to go claim my lover.

"I have an appointment, Miguel," I said abruptly. "Good seeing you." I headed toward Jack, leaving Miguel behind.

As I got closer to Jack and Danny, Mrs. Flores came into view. She'd been standing behind the stone angel all along. I felt relieved, and foolish for being jealous to begin with.

Jack said his good-byes to the Flores mother and son, and we climbed into the pickup. As we pulled away from the curb, I glanced back at the tent, which trembled in the wind as though it were sobbing. I had the awful feeling that everyone was abandoning Eddie, leaving him there in the freezing wind before he was tucked away under a blanket of earth. For a moment, I thought about asking Jack to turn around and take me back so I could stand over Eddie until the cemetery crew finished burying him. But I knew the impulse was ridiculous. Eddie's spirit wasn't at the grave. It was soaring above us in the bright warmth of heaven.

Jack was thoughtful on the ride back to St. John's. We rode along quietly for a long time.

"You said Eddie's rosary ring came from Lourdes?" Jack finally said.

I nodded. "It was his dream come true. His favorite movie was *Song of Bernadette*."

The old film starred Jean Simmons as little Bernadette, visited by the Virgin Mary in a grotto where garbage was dumped. Vincent Price played the disbelieving bishop who finally consecrated the ground once a spring in the grotto started curing sick people who bathed in it. I'd watched it with Eddie a dozen times over the years.

"Did he bathe in the waters?" Jack said.

The question brought back to me the sad reality of Eddie's self-division. "Yes," I said. "He wanted to be cured of his homosexuality."

Jack laughed, cracked the window, and lit a cigarette. "What a wasted pilgrimage."

The response relieved me, and I realized that I'd been afraid that he actually might have approved of Eddie's mission.

"So you don't think we need to be cured?" I said.

He shook his head and glanced at me. "The church doesn't either, you know."

"No, it just says we're disordered. Like Frankenstein monsters."

"Who cares?" Jack said.

"I guess it's another one of those silly teachings in the church's hierarchy of doctrines?"

"That's right." Jack squeezed my leg reassuringly.

He seemed so confident in this belief and so sexy to me in that moment that I didn't want to argue. Why be a crusader? If I just gave myself to Jack, my worries would vanish. And wasn't love all about surrender?

So much for my understanding of love! What did I know about how healthy relationships work? Nothing. Even though I'd counseled couples for fifteen years, following all the principles I'd learned in ministry classes, I didn't have a clue. We were special. Our love fell under no rubric. We were guided by the stars.

4

A FEW DAYS after the funeral, I went on my weekly trek to visit my mother. Oncoming traffic was heavy as I entered the turnpike.

When my cell phone rang, I dug it out of my coat pocket and said hello.

"Hey," Jack responded. "No marriage counseling tonight. How about meeting earlier? Five or so. I could swing by your mother's. Maybe she'd like to come to dinner with us."

The idea of my lover in the same room with my mother made me uncomfortable. Maybe she'd know her son the priest was in love and fall to pieces. "She doesn't like Mexican," I said.

"We could go somewhere else. Hamburgers would be fine."

"I don't think so," I hedged. "A whole day with her is long enough."

"She's not gonna look at me and *know*."

"That's not why," I lied, apparently unconvincingly because Jack chuckled. I ignored it. "I'll just meet you at Santa Rosa's."

In my old neighborhood, the wood frame houses seemed to huddle in the cold. Plastic reindeer and Santas had disappeared from the frozen yards, leaving behind garden gnomes and the occasional concrete statue of the Virgin Mary.

I parked on the street in front of my mother's house, got out, and headed up the sidewalk that my brother Jim must have cleared. In the yard, the Virgin extended chipped hands over the snow-covered flowerbed at the base of the long concrete porch. My mother kept the simple house in tip-top shape. Clean vinyl siding wrapped the walls. Shuttered windows sparkled. A new layer of shingles lay flat and even on the roof and central dormer. Built by my old man with his own hands, the house looked better than it had during his life. Joe Seib had worked as hard as he drank, but he was no perfectionist.

The front door opened before I could ring the bell. My petite mother smiled at me through the storm door and opened it. I stepped in and hugged her. She was soft as a rag doll in her velour sweatsuit.

"Why don't you wear your Roman collar?" she said, drawing back to inspect my sweater. "You could wear it underneath. Father Dennis does." Short permed curls framed her round face. Her skin was remarkably smooth for a woman over seventy. Her gray eyes flickered with pride behind large glasses. I was her son, the priest!

"Father Dennis probably sleeps in his Roman collar," I said. I kissed her forehead and sat on the couch, and she went to get me some coffee from the kitchen.

Jack was probably right to laugh at my worries. She would never suspect anything between us. But I felt that I had to protect her, the way I'd protected her my whole life from the one fact about me that would devastate her—an irrelevant fact since the day of my ordination, when I had formally vowed to remain celibate for the rest of my life. It suddenly hit me how preposterous my fantasy had been about me and Jack living like a regular couple in our own house, inviting our friends to cookouts.

My mother returned with a mug of coffee. She set it on a coaster on the coffee table and settled in her upholstered rocking chair across from me. A prayer book rested on the table by the chair. Near it, a pile of blue rosary beads lay on a crocheted doily. Framed photos of my brother Jim and my sister Ronny with their spouses and kids crowded the wall next to her. A photo of me, taken on ordination day, hung between mounted candles on the wall above her. My gold chasuble and solemn, golden looks reminded me now of a ciborium, and so I was then—a human ciborium, full of Divine power. I'd felt exactly that holy on ordination day in St. Peter's Basilica, the mighty matrix of the holy Catholic Church. That day was the culmination of ten years of seminary training, from high school seminary to college seminary to theological studies in Rome.

"How was church this morning?" I said, sipping my coffee. My mother never missed daily mass.

She shook her head sadly. "Martha Gerhardt was there. She came in from Wamego because it was a memorial mass for Father Edward. It's his birthday. I felt so sorry for her. I can't imagine losing a son. And a priest! Why would he kill himself?"

"Who knows?" I said evasively.

By now, everyone knew how Eddie died. The archbishop had directed his priests to tell the truth when asked, but they were not to make public statements about Eddie's suicide.

My mother sighed. "Well, it's just a shame. Remember when you and Father Edward played that duet at St. John's? During intermission of the school play? You were both so young and skinny. It was the music from the movie with Robert Redford. *The Sting,* wasn't it?"

I pictured Eddie at the piano in a striped shirt with a banded collar, garters on the sleeves. He would turn his head and beam at the audience the way Norma Zimmer had on the Lawrence Welk show, his favorite Saturday night entertainment. Next to him, I squeaked out the Joplin ragtime piece on my clarinet.

"Father Dennis has been leading a rosary every morning before mass," my mother continued. "We're praying for the Gerhardts. Martha said they ordered a beautiful headstone. The Blessed Virgin is etched on it, and it has two attached vases. When it comes in, I want you to drive out to Wamego with me and put flowers on the grave. You could bless it, too, honey."

Depressed by the subject, I shifted the conversation to something trivial. We chatted until I finished my coffee, and then I went to my old bedroom and changed into the work clothes I kept in a dresser. I'd promised to paint a basement closet so Jim wouldn't have to. Mom expected him to be her handyman, never dreaming of asking her son the priest to sully his consecrated hands with menial tasks. She'd put up a fight when I insisted on painting the closet. I have to admit, I'd come to expect being on such a pedestal. It was all I knew. Only occasional twinges of guilt about Jim prompted me to resist.

Mom's finished basement contained a big space divided into a kitchen and living room, two small bedrooms, a tiny room used as a closet, and a bath. An adjacent utility room still housed the furnace, hot-water heater, washer, and dryer.

Dad had miscalculated when he designed the stairs to the basement: each step was only eight inches wide and padded with treacherous carpet. On coming home from the neighborhood tavern one night, he'd attempted to steal down the stairs and sleep off the binge without grief from Mom, but he slipped on the narrow steps, slid down the staircase on his back, and crashed through the door leading into the apartment. A fight between Dad and Mom had ensued, punctuated by shattering dishes, hurled by Dad against the kitchen wall.

Used to the narrow stairs, I hurried down them without a thought, entered the apartment, and passed through the living room to the walk-in closet. I spent the rest of the morning and several hours after lunch taping, priming, and painting the room with the powder-blue hue Mom had picked. I applied the paint carefully, with even strokes, losing myself in the quiet rhythm of the brush, thinking of Jack.

At four o'clock, I was finished. After cleaning the brushes and changing my clothes, I sat with Mom in the kitchen until it was time to meet Jack. She never expected me to stay for dinner on my Thursday visits because I usually had work to finish before a Friday staff meeting. I was rinsing my mug at the sink when the doorbell rang. I figured it was a neighborhood kid selling candy or magazines for a school fund-raiser.

But when I opened the door and flicked on the porch light, I found Jack grinning inanely at me through the storm door. My stomach tensed.

"I thought you were going to wait for me," I said as Jack stepped in.

"Surprise!" Jack said, kissing me on the cheek.

I pulled away and glanced toward the kitchen.

"Who is it, honey?" Mom called.

"Hey, Mrs. Seib," Jack answered. "It's Jack Canston." Jack winked at me and walked into the kitchen.

I followed, panic rising in my chest. Why had he shown up? Was he teasing me? Was it some kind of test?

"Good lands, Jack!" Mom hugged him. "Here, take off your coat."

When he did, his Roman collar appeared. It had the effect of the star over Bethlehem for her. Her gray eyes brightened. "So you got ordained. In Montana, right? Here, sit down. Let me get you some coffee."

Jack pulled out the chair at the head of the table. He threw me a playful glance as I settled in the chair next to him.

"I wondered what happened to you," Mom said, handing Jack his coffee. "Chris said he lost track of you after you graduated from St. John's. He sure loved going out to Montana and spending time with your family. How are they doing? I think I met your parents at your graduation."

"They're good," Jack said. "Could I get a little sugar?"

Mom scowled at her own forgetfulness and ran after the sugar.

After spooning some into his coffee, Jack turned to my mother again. "How have you been doing? You look great. You haven't changed a bit since we were in high school."

"Oh," Mom said, dismissing the compliment with a wave of her hand.

"The house looks just the same, too. Just like I remember it when Chris invited me over for weekends."

I remembered my initial embarrassment at bringing the son of a suburban lawyer to the modest home of an alcoholic carpenter who'd dropped out of high school. But Jack's piety had blinded him to what he called "worldly distinctions."

"What brings you back here?" Mom said.

I waited with interest for the response, but Jack only repeated his rehearsed statement about Montana's lonely distances and the need for a change.

"Isn't it horrible about Father Edward?" Mom said, out of the blue.

The playfulness in Jack's eyes vanished. "Yes."

"His funeral mass was just beautiful. You must have been one of the priests? There were so many up at the altar. That was such a beautiful sight."

"It was beautiful," Jack said, solemnly. "Faith is all we have. Life doesn't end. It begins. Christ tells us that."

Mom nodded. "I just don't understand why a priest would want to kill himself. It's a sacrilege."

"It is," Jack agreed, his tone suddenly harsh and his dark eyes full of fierceness. "I think it's the worst kind of sin."

This was too much for me. I started to defend Eddie but realized I couldn't without exposing him to more abuse. So I kept my mouth shut.

Even Mom seemed a little alarmed at Jack's hostility. She moved to safer ground. "A priest can be closer to our Lord. And God gives him such strength. I think Father Edward was a very holy priest. He brought me back a rosary from Lourdes. I think of him now every time I use it."

The subject of Lourdes seemed to calm Jack. He asked to see the rosary, and Mom retrieved the beads I'd seen in the living room and entrusted them to his hand. Jack studied them sadly. "I'd like to go to Lourdes," he said.

"Me, too," said Mom, reverently. "Maybe I will before I die." She glanced imploringly at me. "Wouldn't you like to go back, honey?"

I remembered with pain Eddie's excitement as he left our hotel room to find the cure he longed for. "Sure," I answered, perfunctorily.

Mom brought out some brochures of Lourdes she'd ordered. She commented longingly on the photos of the grotto where the Virgin Mary had appeared and of the church built near the site in the late nineteenth century. The building reminded me of the Disneyland castle. When she finally exhausted the topic, Jack and I said our goodbyes to her and headed in our separate cars for a Mexican restaurant near Santa Rosa's.

We met in the parking lot and entered the little square building. Recorded mariachi music bounced through speakers. The burly host greeted Jack with recognition. As he led us to a booth near a window, several customers in the crowded dining room smiled and nodded at Jack.

"Looks like you've already made your mark," I said, spreading the linen napkin on my lap.

Jack shrugged. "It's a friendly parish."

I was surprised when the handsome kid from the funeral appeared at our table with some tortilla chips and salsa. He greeted Jack with a grin, nodding to me. A red T-shirt stretched across his meaty chest. His forearm was tattooed with an image of the Virgin of Guadalupe. I stared at it while he took our order.

"*Gracias,* Danny," Jack said, handing him back the menus. "See you tonight at Adoration."

Danny smiled and headed for the kitchen.

It was stupid and petty, but Danny's appearance roused the jealousy I'd felt at the funeral. I wanted to strike out at Jack. "They never get tired of cookie worship?" I blurted, using Corey's term for Eucharistic Adoration.

"Hey, you're talking about the Blessed Sacrament." Jack lit a cigarette, and young Danny scurried back over with an ashtray and then off to another table.

"C'mon, Jack," I said. "They kneel all night in front of a communion wafer displayed in a monstrance. What's the point? Isn't God everywhere?"

Narrowing his eyes in the smoke, Jack stared at me. He turned his head and exhaled away from the table. "You pissed because I came to your mother's?" he said.

"I asked you not to."

He shrugged. "I wanted to show you it was no big deal."

"Why do you have to show me *anything*?" I took a breath, dipped a tortilla chip in the salsa, and ate it. "Okay. I'm listening. What's no big deal?"

Jack leaned forward on the table and stared earnestly at me. "Us. She never has to know a thing. You're a priest. I'm a priest. In public we have a responsibility to shepherd the people. Never to scandalize. In private, we can follow our consciences."

My first impulse was to protest. What about integrity? What about confronting oppression in the church? But my resistance quickly dissolved under his seductive authority, and I actually felt relieved. Jack was right. I could go on protecting Mom's innocence. Jack and I could live out our own romantic dream behind closed doors, just the two of us on an island. We didn't have to bear the social stigma, like some kind of mark of the Devil on our foreheads. We didn't have to give up the only world we'd ever known as holy priests of God.

AFTER DINNER, I accompanied Jack to Santa Rosa's for the benediction service. The sanctuary of the mission-style church glowed with red votive candles that cluttered the side altars. High above the main altar, a spotlight bathed the mosaic image of the Virgin of Guadalupe, appearing to a Mexican peasant on his knees. Sweet incense and the beeswax of candles lingered in the air. Two women mumbled their rosaries in a front pew.

Jack flicked on the sanctuary lights, we entered the sparse sacristy, and Jack retrieved the monstrance from a cupboard. I carried the heavy gold vessel to the altar and then prepared the incense while Jack donned a spotless linen alb and a gold cape. Before long the sounds of footsteps, whispering, and tuning guitars echoed in the sanctuary.

Assuming that I would serve as acolyte, I reached for an alb in the vestment wardrobe.

"Don't worry about it," Jack said. "Danny's coming."

"Oh," I said, disappointed.

I returned the alb and took a seat in one of the front pews, among a dozen kneeling parishioners. Within a few minutes, Danny, his black hair now moussed and gleaming, hurried down the aisle, genuflected devoutly before the tabernacle, and entered the sacristy. The two guitar players began strumming and broke into a Spanish song when Danny appeared again in the sanctuary, followed by Jack. Wearing a surplice and cassock, Danny swung the censer, clinking the chain against the casing as they processed to the altar steps and knelt.

When the hymn ended, Jack proceeded through the litany in good, clear Spanish. Evidently his years at Monterrey had made him fluent.

When he finished the final litany, he reverently retrieved a communion host from the tabernacle and inserted it in the monstrance. Wrapping a gold mantle around his shoulders and around the base of the monstrance, he raised the bright vessel over the worshippers, who knelt in silence, striking their breasts with their fists. Three times, Jack pivoted with the monstrance, blessing each section of the church, while Danny swung the censer in the direction of the sacred host. Smoke curled into a cloud around Jack, like the cloud around God on Mount Sinai.

At the end of the service, Jack placed the monstrance on the altar where parishioners would adore it in shifts throughout the night. As he put everything back in order, Danny tagged after him like a puppy. I stayed in my pew, leaving them to their work. Before Danny left, he dropped to his knees in front of Jack, who laid his hands in blessing upon the sweet boy's head.

The picture of Danny and Jack stayed in my mind all the way back to St. John's.

IN BED JACK drew his arm over my chest and kissed my ear. "Still mad at me?" he said.

"No," I whispered.

"Why are you so quiet?"

I couldn't bring myself to confess my ridiculous jealousy. I turned and kissed him. He climbed on top of me, grabbed my wrists, and stretched out my arms until our bodies formed a cross. He sucked my neck and lips and tongue. The weight of his body practically crushed the breath out of me. His engorged dick bore into my crotch, as though it might tear through my skin. I opened for him, waited for the hard flesh, and when it entered me, felt the ecstasy of true adoration.

THE NEXT MORNING, sunlight flooded Archbishop Koch's spacious office on the main floor. Theology tomes crowded the floor-to-ceiling shelves, except on one large wall that displayed a nineteenth-century painting of the Virgin Mary being carried into heaven by two angels. A book rack containing church directories and ministry manuals sat on one side of his large desk, and a computer terminal on the other. In the middle, a carved crucifix in a stand rose above a neat desk calendar.

I sat in a cozy armchair, waiting for the archbishop to bring us coffee from the little kitchen next to his office.

He entered with two steaming mugs embossed with the diocesan coat of arms. Handing one to me, he closed the door before sitting in an armchair across from me.

As always, he was the picture of order. His clerical shirt and dark trousers were pressed and spotless. His black oxfords gleamed as he crossed his bony legs. His bald pate and closely shaved face shone. The bags beneath his kind eyes suggested a sleepless night.

"I need your advice, Chris," he said. "I've been stewing over this." Sighing, he rose and retrieved a file from a cabinet in the corner of the room. He pulled out an envelope and handed it to me. The envelope bore the archbishop's typed address and a canceled postage stamp. There was no return address. The envelope had been opened with a paper knife.

"Go ahead," the archbishop said. "Read the letter."

I pulled out the letter and read the note, printed by a computer:

Dear Excellency,

I never came forward, I know. But who would have believed someone like me? I want you to know now, though. Father Edward deserved to die and he knew it. I carried the shame of what he did to me around like some kind of leprosy. Now the shame is over. Alleluia. God smites the wicked. By that I mean pastors who take advantage of their sheep.

I'm telling you this now, so you don't make some kind of martyr out of him. I'm the martyr. Now I'm vindicated.

"My God," I said. "This is sick." I glanced up at the archbishop, whose brow was furrowed. "It's a lie, Archbishop. An unsigned letter like this . . ."

"How can we know it's a lie?" the archbishop said quietly.

I wondered if Eddie's suicide note had contained information prompting the archbishop to believe the stuff in this unsigned letter. I had no way of knowing, because the archbishop had stuck to the refusal he'd made to discuss the note's contents with me. But if Eddie had confessed to something like this, why would the archbishop have any doubts at all? "Is there any past evidence against Eddie in your files?" I finally said.

The archbishop shook his head. "No, nothing. But I've only been in the archdiocese for five years. What if Archbishop Mallory held something back? In the old days . . ." Koch hesitated. "In the old days, bishops made mistakes. They thought they were acting for the good of the church."

I shook my head. "Whoever wrote this letter wants us to think that he was some altar boy that Eddie abused. But I knew Eddie. He wasn't a pedophile. I promise you. This is some demented parishioner that Eddie crossed. Or maybe . . ." I hesitated to voice my true suspicion, but finally thought, what the hell, tell him the truth. "Maybe this is a jilted lover. I know Eddie was gay. He was determined to be celibate, but anyone can fall."

The archbishop raised his hands to stop me from going on. "I don't want a defense of homosexuality. Certainly not when it comes to my priests. Cardinal Ramirez is right."

"What?" I said. "None of your priests can be gay?"

"Please, Chris. This is not the time to distinguish between one scandal and another. The person who wrote this letter could do a lot of damage in the diocese."

For a second I was too mad to speak. Then I imagined Jack laughing at me, saying that I was making a big deal out of nothing. And maybe my skin *was* getting too thin. Maybe with Jack next to me, I could blow the archbishop off without a thought. But in that moment, I couldn't. "So why are you showing me this?" I said.

"I'm asking you before anything comes to light. You and Edward were friends—are you aware of *any* inappropriate relationships that he might have had?" He seemed to hold his breath as he waited for an answer.

"No," I said. "None."

Relieved, he folded up the letter.

Jack Canston's Journal

January 6

The miraculous waters of Lourdes. Can't get that holy spring out of my mind. Little Bernadette Soubirous kneeling before the Virgin in the grotto. Come on, waters! Wash us all. Cure us all. Blind people say they were cured at Lourdes. Crippled people. Don't I know what it's like to want a cure! To get the monkey off my back. To chase off the nightmares. Maybe nightmares are worse than a physical disease. A cripple can have a tranquil soul. A cripple maybe can keep it all separate. Holy Church there. My life here. A cripple maybe always sees the church like some kind of shelter. Or maybe it's just resignation that keeps him from screaming at God. Where are you, God! Where are you!

Santa Rosa's has got a mess of troubled people. Struggling to make ends meet. To keep the family together. And drugs, drugs as always. They need me closer. The people need me. I have a duty to be there.

But I need his arms. I need to be inside him. And sometimes I want to hurt him because I need him. Then ramming him is like ramming . . . the fucking demons.

Cast them out, Christ! You've got the power. Isn't that what I preached about today? On the Feast of the Epiphany? The three wise men saw the power in you and dropped to their knees. Well, then, cure me, Christ. Damn it! Cure me!

5

THE NEXT MORNING when I checked my e-mail I found a message from the archbishop, who had left before dawn for a conference on the west coast. He instructed me to head to Eddie's rectory and take a look around for anything incriminating. The housekeeper would let me in.

I wondered what the point was. If I did find something scandalous, what was I supposed to do? Just turn it over to the archbishop? Never. I almost decided that I would lie to the archbishop—tell him I'd carried out his orders and come up empty-handed. But on reflection, I changed my mind. This was a perfect opportunity for me to search for and hide anything that could be used to taint Eddie's memory.

I got my coat, told my secretary where I was going, and climbed down the front stairs to the underground garage and got in my

Honda. Even with the heat turned up, I was all the way to the interstate before I stopped shivering.

In the cold, frozen snow still lay on the ground. I gazed absently over the white fields as I drove, thinking of Eddie. I remembered how excited he'd been to get assigned to the historic St. Mary's. "It's the oldest German church in northeast Kansas," he'd bragged to me over a mug of beer one night. "The reredos comes from Bavaria!" I remembered him prancing around in an alpine hat and lederhosen at the parish's annual Oktoberfest. When the band played a polka, he yanked a hefty woman to her feet and danced her across the floor of the church basement.

When I reached St. Mary's, I pulled up in front of the rectory next door. The wide brick house was built in the thirties, in the prairie design created by Frank Lloyd Wright. Its long, flowing lines gave it a comfortable, open feel. Of course, Eddie would have preferred a Victorian mansion with a turret, but he said the Romanesque church compensated for the "modern" residence, as he'd once referred to it with mock disdain.

Also built in the prairie style, the garage where Eddie had killed himself sat back from the house, at the end of a long driveway. I wondered if the Plymouth was still inside or if Eddie's family had taken it away.

In front of the house, a teenage boy was shoveling the walk. He wore headphones over his black stocking cap. He removed them when I tapped him on the shoulder.

"It's sure cold out here," I said. "Hope the parish is paying you time and a half."

"It's for a tuition discount at Good Shepherd," the boy said, with reserve. A fringe of down gave him what looked like a Kool-Aid moustache. "My mom made a deal with Father Edward." He nodded toward the two-story houses across the street.

I glanced up. A woman in a blue sweatshirt watched from a picture window. I waved and she waved back.

"What's your name?" I said.

"George Madson."

"I'm Father Chris." I stuck out my hand. George raised his nylon mitten, managing an awkward handshake. "I'm sorry about Father Edward," I said. "I'll bet he appreciated your work out here."

George shrugged and lowered his blue eyes. When he looked up again his gaze was intense. "I thought suicide was a mortal sin," he said, with a strange hostility.

"We can't judge Father Edward. Who knows what was in his mind? He must have been really depressed."

The boy nodded dismissively and wiped his nose with his mitten.

His hostility made me think of the anonymous letter, and a disturbing thought came to my head. I wanted to brush it aside, but I had to ask, no matter how unfounded my fear might be. "Did you spend a lot of time over here? With Father Edward?"

"I guess."

"Helping out with chores?"

"Sure."

I put my hand on his shoulder. "Is there anything you want to say? Did Father Edward ever do anything . . . that bothered you?"

George jerked away. "He was a priest."

"Priests aren't perfect. They can do things that are wrong."

"I gotta finish this," George said. Replacing his headphones, he resumed shoveling.

I pulled my card from my wallet and tapped him on the back. He removed his headphones again and took the card.

"If you need to talk about anything, call me," I said. "I mean it." I waved at his mother and walked to the front door of the rectory.

Pam, the housekeeper, answered the doorbell. She was a wiry woman with her dirty blond hair pulled back in a ponytail. She wore a hot-pink sweatshirt, silk-screened with an American flag. She smelled like nicotine. The archbishop had called her to let her know I was coming to retrieve some diocesan files and some personal things for Eddie's family. She led me down the darkened oak floor of the foyer and opened one of the curtained French doors leading into the pastor's office. I followed her in.

I scanned the heavy, upholstered chairs and oak antiques in the large, well-lit room. On a table against the wall, the Infant of Prague stared placidly from inside his glass dome. Everything seemed so perfectly in order. I wondered if Eddie had written the suicide note on the large desk in the corner of the room. The note must have been handwritten. He hated computers. They were too modern and ugly for him.

"I still can't believe it, Father," Pam said. "What is this world coming to? Baby killers and terrorists just go scot-free. I think that's why Father Edward did it. He couldn't stand it anymore!" The outburst set off a smoker's cough, and she cleared her throat. "Let me know if you need anything," she said, leaving the room.

I searched the drawers of Eddie's desk, not even sure what I was looking for. Books on gay themes? Notes from lovers?

But I found nothing unusual in the desk. Just the usual parish directories, sermon notes, and stationery. In a closet, I sorted through coats, cassocks, and a few boxes without turning up anything suspicious.

I found Pam in the kitchen and let her know I needed to see Eddie's bedroom. She led me up the carpeted stairs and opened the first door we came to in the hallway on the second floor. I thanked her by way of dismissal, and she disappeared.

I'd been to the rectory plenty of times but never in Eddie's room. In the middle of it sat a four-poster bed with a canopy. The floral fabric matched the drapes, wallpaper, and wingback chairs. Over-the-top was Eddie's style. On the wall hung a painting of Our Lady of Lourdes, standing in a grotto niche, her hands folded. A large crucifix hung above the bed.

On the nightstand, I found laminated holy cards, a rosary, and a half-full water glass. Pam evidently found the room too sacred to disturb in any way. Even Eddie's plaid flannel slippers still lay on the rug—the same kind he'd worn in high school. I checked the nightstand drawer and found aspirin, cough drops, playing cards, and another rosary.

Under the bed, I found nothing but an empty suitcase. I went to the closet and was not surprised to find it carefully organized, shirts on one side, trousers on the other, shoes in a rack on the floor. I sorted quickly through Eddie's clothes, choking up when I came across the lederhosen and suspenders. I found nothing unusual there or in the drawers of the tall chest standing in an alcove.

At a loss for where to look next, I glanced up at the family photographs that took up a whole wall, a wedding portrait of Eddie's parents in the center. His father looked as severe as I had remembered him from his occasional visits to St. John's. According to Eddie, one method old Gerhardt had used to make a man of his sissy son was to smear Eddie's own feces on his face and lock him in a closet.

I was heading for the door when, on an impulse, I turned to the bed. Flipping back the comforter, I slipped my hand under the mattress and pulled out two glossy skin magazines. I smiled at gentle Eddie's tastes. In one magazine the models were dressed like cops and firemen. In the other they posed on motorcycles, in studded leather jackets.

I slipped the magazines into the briefcase I had brought and went down to the kitchen. I found Pam smoking on the back porch.

"I'm taking off, Pam."

"You get what you needed, Father?" She stubbed out her cigarette in an ashtray.

I nodded.

"Has the archbishop chosen a replacement for Father Edward?" she asked.

"He's still reviewing possibilities."

"No one can really replace him," she said, sadly. "He was one of a kind!"

I agreed, smiling.

The sidewalk to the street was perfectly clear. George was busy shoveling the driveway. When he glanced up there was no trace in his expression of the hostility I'd perceived. I waved, dismissing my worries. Eddie had probably gotten on his case once or twice. Or maybe George was just a normal, malcontented teenager.

THAT EVENING, I stood in my living room, scooping a dead angelfish from my new aquarium. The dead fish was the first of what would be many casualties of my inexperience with aquatic life.

Jack sat on the couch smoking, his stockinged feet propped on the coffee table. We'd just finished a pizza I'd heated in the staff kitchen. The dirty plates sat on the table in the corner. I carried the fish to the bathroom and flushed it. Then I returned to the living room and sat next to him.

"I went to Eddie's rectory today," I said. "The archbishop sent me to look around."

"For what?"

"Anything incriminating. He's worried about a scandal." I told him about the anonymous letter.

Jack's reaction seemed normal enough. He looked concerned that some lunatic would cause problems for the diocese. He lit a cigarette and brooded as I talked about my trip to the rectory, finally getting up and gazing out the window, as though he was too restless to sit still. My report about the magazines didn't seem to faze him. I told him I planned to get rid of them and say nothing to Koch about them.

"So he expected you to look for evidence and destroy it?" he finally said.

"Or bring it back and let him destroy it. He pissed me off today." I told him about Koch's comments.

"He's just upset by the suicide," Jack said distractedly.

"I knew you'd say that."

He turned away from the window. Wheels were clearly spinning in his head. "That's all you found—magazines?"

"Yes," I said, puzzled by his sudden intensity. "Why? Do you think the rumors about a lover are true?"

"Who knows?" he said.

Agitated, he rubbed his face as though a dead insect were stuck to it. He turned back to the window and stared out. "This is getting to me. I keep seeing Eddie locked inside his car. I keep wondering if he died in the state of grace."

"Of course he did!" I said, trying not to sound impatient at such a ridiculous fear. I could see the idea really bothered Jack. I went to him and wrapped my arms around him, looking over his shoulder at the starry sky through the window. "This is taking a toll on everybody. How could it not? I mean, Eddie must have been miserable. We did nothing to help him."

Jack nodded. He picked up my hand and kissed it.

For a while, we quietly watched TV. Jack sat with his arms folded, clearly still troubled, his thoughts miles away. Then all of a sudden, he stood up.

"I've gotta get out of this building," he said. "I'm going running."

"It's freezing."

"I don't care." He started out of the room.

"Wait," I said, worried about him. "I'll go with you."

I changed into my sweats, grabbed a jacket, and met him at his apartment. As he sat on the sofa tying his shoes, I noticed his wood carvings in the wastebasket, lying on top of newspapers and cigarette butts.

"Why are you throwing these out?" I said, pulling out the elk.

"Leave it there."

"It's beautiful, Jack." I wasn't much on animal sculptures, but I wasn't lying. Even though the figure was only eight inches tall, the hooves and antlers were finely detailed.

"I don't want it," he snapped. "I threw it out for a reason."

"What reason?" I said, perplexed.

"My own fucking reason. Okay?" He got up, grabbed the figure from my hand, and dropped it into the wastebasket.

I stared at him, confused.

"Look," he said, suddenly contrite. "I'm sorry. It's all too much for me. The move. The new parish. Eddie's death. It's just a lot."

I nodded, forgiving him. Just like that. It's what you do when you love someone, I thought, as ridiculously inept as I was in the ways of mature love. He kissed me. We grabbed our jackets and scarves and headed outside.

Under a full moon, we jogged along the old cross-country course, now covered in snow. Fences and trees outlined the invisible path that we knew so well. We'd run it together hundreds of times in high school. I hoped Jack would take comfort in the familiar path. We ran without talking, our breath steaming the air. When we finished the two-mile track, Jack turned to me, lowering the scarf from his mouth.

"Let's run to the park," he said.

"We should stay on the property," I objected. "It's too dark to run on the road."

"We can run on the shoulder."

"The snow's piled up on it."

"There's a full moon. We'll be fine," Jack coaxed. "Come on. There's no traffic out there."

Against my better judgment, I gave in, thinking Jack needed to work off his restlessness. We crunched across the field to the road and ran uphill to the highway, a mile away. Traffic was light. After a few cars sped by, we jogged across the road and continued for half a mile, to the entrance of Wyandotte County Park, where the cross-country team used to run timed sprints.

We followed the lamp-lit road that wound through the park. Around us, the moonlight revealed the silhouettes of bare branches, picnic tables, and stone stoves.

All of a sudden, Jack picked up speed, sprinting ahead of me.

"What are you doing?" I shouted after him.

He didn't answer. As he passed a picnic shelter, he cut off the road toward a cluster of trees. I figured he'd gone to relieve himself.

I walked the rest of the way to the shelter and waited there. Soon I was shivering. I rubbed my arms and paced in the cold. "Are you okay?" I shouted.

There was no response. Worried, I jogged across the snowy clearing to the trees, where I stopped and looked around. When I ventured farther into the wooded area, I saw a figure sitting on a fallen tree. I shouted again, but Jack didn't answer and I approached him. He was staring at the moon.

"Why didn't you answer?" I said. "What's wrong?"

"It's beautiful, isn't it?" Jack said, entranced.

At a loss for what to say or do, I sat down next to him. It was clear now that whatever bothered him was much bigger then he'd let on. It wasn't Eddie's death. It wasn't the stress of a new parish. It was an old wound, not a recent one. And it was deep.

I felt helpless. I sat there shivering next to him for ten minutes, not once opening my mouth, hoping he was pulling himself together.

Suddenly, he stood up and walked away.

I followed him, astounded that he'd just left me there. When I reached him, it was clear that he'd resolved nothing. He still seemed oblivious to me, even desperate. But I couldn't get him to talk, and so I just trudged alongside him all the way back to the entrance of the park.

After we exited and walked along the road for a few yards, we came to a heap near the shoulder.

"Look," Jack said. "It's a dog."

We stooped down to examine it. Blood was oozing from the head of the large, black mutt. Jack petted the dog tenderly. "Christ. What asshole would do this? What fucking asshole would just hit a dog and leave it here?"

"Maybe they didn't know they hit it," I said.

"Bullshit!" Jack shouted, furious. "Don't you think you'd know if you hit a dog this size?" He continued to pet the dog compulsively. "Why in the hell did they do it? So goddamned cruel."

His agitation scared me. He seemed ready to break into sobs, but I was afraid to comfort him.

"We can't just leave it out here," he said, appearing to gain control of himself. "We've gotta bury it."

"The ground's frozen. Let's just drag it off the road and call the county pound."

"I'm not leaving it in a ditch. We'll go get my truck and take it back to St. John's. We can burn it."

"Where?" I was incredulous.

"On the property. We'll find a place."

I could see there was no stopping him. We ran all the way back to St. John's, got in the truck, and returned to the spot. The whole way, Jack moved with a frightening intensity, oblivious to my presence. When we reached the dog, Jack stopped his truck in the middle of the road without turning on his emergency signals. I scanned the road nervously for oncoming cars as he removed his sweatshirt and wrapped it around the dog's bloody head. We hoisted the carcass into the bed of the truck, climbed in, and drove back to St. John's in silence.

Jack followed the drive around the complex to the southwest side of the property, where he pulled off the road and crossed the field, stopping at the handball court, which hadn't been used in a decade. We got out and laid the dog on the concrete. Jack retrieved a plastic container of gasoline from the bed of the truck and dowsed the animal. He made the sign of the cross over it before flinging the lit match. The carcass exploded into flames.

In the heat of the fire, the acrid smell of burning hair and flesh in our nostrils, Jack let me hold his hand. In the flames, I could see tears on his face. We stood like that a long time. Finally we sat on the concrete to wait for the fire to burn down. Jack never took his eyes from it. When the flames dwindled, I finally coaxed him to leave. The holocaust seemed to purge his wild intensity. He was sober and calm. It didn't seem to occur to him that there would still be remains to dispose of. I didn't remind him. I just planned to take care of them the next day, which I did.

When we crawled into my bed, Jack clung to me. He fell asleep right away. But as exhausted as I was, I lay awake, my mind racing. What was wrong with him? What had brought on his insane behavior? What was I supposed to do about it?

I might have come to my senses there in the bed. I might have listened to the sensible, mature voice in my head trying to break through this adolescent fantasy, but I had nothing to replace it. No new prospect on the horizon to stir my passion. I deserved passion, after all, after years of deprivation.

I was still wide awake two hours later, when the phone rang in my living room. I hurried to answer it before it woke up Jack. When I picked up the receiver and said hello, no one spoke. Then the line went dead.

6

"I FEEL SILLY now, Chris. I don't know what I expected you to find in Edward's rectory." The archbishop looked up at me from behind his large desk. His brown, sad, hooded eyes reminded me of a basset hound's. "Do you think I failed him?"

"Maybe we all did." I decided I had been too hard on him. But I had no qualms about telling him I'd found nothing in my search. I'd tossed the magazines in the Dumpster behind the dining hall—along with the charred remains of the dog.

I left the archbishop and went to my office. I spent the morning making out the monthly schedule of the events at the center, resisting the urge to call Jack. Yesterday, the day after the dog incident, I'd called him five or six times. He finally ordered me to stop, assuring me that he was fine.

But I couldn't get his bizarre behavior out of my mind. I needed to talk to someone about it.

At noon, I walked down the hall to Sister Alberta Smith's office. Alberta counseled pregnant teens and made referrals to a support facility run by Catholic Charities. She was from the old school of nuns: no-nonsense, dedicated, and loyal to the church. But we'd become good friends over the past two years, and I trusted her.

I found her at her desk on the phone. She looked up at me with her clear hazel eyes and gestured for me to sit down on a lime-green couch. On the wall behind her hung a poster with the words "Bloom Where You Are Planted" scribbled above a sunflower growing from a boulder. The tall metal file cabinet near the desk was plastered with photos of her nieces and nephews. On top of the cabinet was a framed picture of the gospel choir she sang in.

"Now, you treat her right, Mary," Alberta commanded, adjusting the short veil on the crown of her head. Her retro-Afro stuck up in front of it. Always complaining of her chilly office, she wore a bulky ski sweater over her broad shoulders. "This girl needs some loving care," she continued. "She just turned fourteen, and she hasn't made any decision about the baby." She issued a series of instructions before hanging up and turning to me. "You look like crap. Didn't you sleep last night?"

"Not really," I sighed. "How about lunch? I'll tell you all my woes at Wendy's. My treat."

Alberta affectionately smirked. "Oh, big spender."

"Can we take your car? I'm not up to driving."

"You're gonna let *me* drive? Honey, you must be bad off."

I smiled. She was right. Her tailgating and quick turns got on my nerves. But today I had problems to distract me.

As we rode along Highway 24 in Alberta's old Volkswagen Beetle, I wondered how much to tell Alberta about Jack. She pulled no punches when it came to giving advice, and I wasn't sure how much advice I wanted.

Wendy's was in the suburban fast-food strip about five miles down the road. We pulled into the crowded parking lot, went in, and waited in a long line. When we finally got our food, we carried it to the last available table.

Alberta said grace. Then she unwrapped her hamburger and took a bite. "Now," she said with her mouth full, "What's wrong?"

I decided to lay everything on the table. "I'm in love," I said.

Alberta's dark eyebrows arched in genuine surprise.

"It's Jack."

"Jack Canston?" she said with surprise. "He just got here."

I shrugged. "I fell in love with him in high school. Only I didn't call it that. Now I know what it is."

Alberta chewed, looking disturbed. "How far has it gone?"

"Please!" I laughed at her old-fashioned morality. "Let's just say it's gone way beyond first base."

She shook her head in disapproval. "So, what about Jack? How does he feel?"

I shrugged and picked up a french fry. "The same, I guess."

"You guess?"

"He initiated it. He's—I don't know—broken. He needs me. Back in high school, he was the rock. And talk about disciplined. We followed his regimen for sanctity to a T. Fasted, prayed, mortified our flesh."

"So, what happened to his ambitions?"

"He grew up," I said, annoyed by her accusatory tone. "We both grew up. Sanctity is more complicated than we thought." I sat back in my chair and sighed. I didn't have the energy to defend myself. "I don't know what happened to him, Alberta. He's as pious as ever. But . . ."

She eyed me sternly. "But he's thrown celibacy out the door. And so have you."

"I've kept my vow all these years!" I snapped.

"Until now," she added judgmentally.

"Yes," I admitted. "Until now."

"And this affair doesn't sit well with you. You have a conscience. What about him?"

"He wouldn't consider leaving the priesthood, if that's what you mean. His holy calling in the one, true church."

"It's your calling, too."

I was silent. I couldn't disagree, could I? Jack had said the same thing. And Jack and I were determined to live out our callings together—as lovers. But I couldn't bring myself to say that to Alberta. I could see she wouldn't hear it.

"What's wrong with him?" Alberta's tone softened. "You said he was broken."

My mouth full, I lifted my hands to express my cluelessness. "Something traumatic happened to him," I finally said. "I don't know what. He's edgy, restless." I described the scene with the dog.

Alberta listened attentively, clearly not liking what she heard. "You're messing with fire, Chris." She patted my hand on the table. "You can't fix whatever is wrong with him. Maybe he does love you, but he's desperate. You want a relationship based on desperation?"

"I'm tired of being alone," I shot back, then lowered my voice when a bald man at the next table looked at me. "I want someone to love. I entered seminary at the age of fourteen, for God's sake. What did I know about myself? When I realized who I was, it was all too late. At least, that's what it felt like. Now I've got a chance to have someone of my own."

"Boo hoo!" Alberta said, showing me no mercy. "You sound like a twelve-year-old whose brother always gets more attention. If you break your vows, you live a lie."

"Promises—not vows," I corrected her, thinking of Jack's careful distinctions. I did sound like I was twelve. And when it came to relationships, I guess I was.

"Whatever." Alberta waved her hand dismissively and wiped her lips with her napkin. "You'll be living a double life."

"What choice do I have?"

Alberta drew back and looked me in the eye. "You can shit or get off the pot."

FOR THE REST of the afternoon, I stewed over Alberta's advice, finally rationalizing that she didn't really understand our situation. At five o'clock, I closed my office door and made my way along the glass corridors to the pool in the west building. The gray twilight on the snow stirred the familiar loneliness that I used to feel years ago as I walked these corridors in the winter.

In the locker room, next to the pool, I changed into my trunks and padded barefoot to the pool, unlocking the steel door and pulling it shut behind me.

I'd finished several laps, when the overhead lights flashed. I lifted my head out of the water.

"Can anyone swim in here?"

Jack's young protégé stood on the deck in jeans and a bulky black sweater. Annoyed to see him, I made myself swim to the side of the pool to greet him. "Hi," I said. "What are you doing here?"

"I came to talk to Father Jack."

"Isn't he at your church?"

"I rode back here with him. He's getting us something to eat."

I climbed out of the pool, and Danny handed me my towel. "You're in pretty good shape, Father. Check out the abs." He patted my stomach. "You must work out a lot."

"Not really," I said, taking in Danny's own muscular physique. "You staying here tonight?" I wondered why Jack couldn't counsel Danny at the church.

He shook his head. "Father Jack is driving me back." His dark eyes scanned the pool. "I've never been here. At St. John's. I've heard about it since I was a kid."

I nodded, drying my chest with the towel. "How old are you?"

"I just turned twenty-three. On the Feast of La Virgen de Guadalupe. This was my birthday present to myself." Danny pulled up the sleeve of his sweater and showed me the tattoo on his forearm.

"I'll bet that's one-of-a-kind," I said.

Danny nodded and smiled, displaying his milk-white teeth. "I was into some bad stuff," he confessed. "The holy Virgin has helped me stay clean. Now I serve at mass, help out around the rectory. Father Jack is cool. He's like my hero."

"He's your spiritual director?"

"Yeah." Danny laughed. "I never thought of it that way. Sounds important."

"It is. Spiritual directors help us find our calling."

"No kidding?" Danny looked impressed. "I think God definitely has a plan for me."

"Of course he does."

"Hey, you mind if I take a dip?" Danny nodded toward the pool.

Before I could respond, he started stripping off his clothes until he stood before me completely naked, stunning and unabashed. He went to the deep end of the pool, flexed his muscular legs, and dived in. His brown body moved through the water with force and grace, the tattoo of the Virgin of Guadalupe surreally flashing as he swam. My eyes glued on him, I waited for him to finish. Then I let him use my towel and chatted with him while he dressed. We walked to the stairs that led up to the dining hall, and I parted from him, afraid Jack would notice my jealousy if I ate with them.

Two hours later, I was starving. When I passed through the chapel on my way back to the west building, I found Jack and Danny kneeling side by side in the dark, reciting the rosary.

IN BED THAT night, I climbed onto Jack and playfully bit his ear.

"Cut it out." Jack winced and shoved me off.

"Sorry." I felt humiliated. "Did Danny wear you out?"

"No. I just don't feel like it. Okay?"

"What if we said a rosary first?" I said, sarcastically. "Maybe that would turn you on."

"Why are you being like this?"

I suddenly felt ashamed. "I don't know. I'm sorry. Really."

" 'Night," Jack said, kissing my hand.

In the middle of the night, Jack shouted in his sleep, "Run! Run!" Then he groaned as if he was in excruciating pain.

I shook him. "Wake up. You're having a nightmare."

He bolted up in bed and looked around, disoriented.

"Bad dream?" I said.

He ran his hands through his hair, reached for a cigarette, and walked out of the bedroom in his pajama bottoms. I heard the living room door open and shut.

I got up and followed him into the hallway, grabbing him by the shoulder. "What's wrong?"

"Just leave me alone, okay?" He jerked away from me and kept walking.

For half an hour I paced and stared at my fish tank, waiting for him to return. Finally, I went out to look for him. In the gallery above the chapel, I gazed down and saw him kneeling completely naked before the tabernacle, his arms stretched out as though he offered himself to torturers.

I'd had enough. If Jack wouldn't tell me what was wrong, I'd find out myself.

Quietly, I left the chapel and walked all the way to the archbishop's office, opening the door with my master key.

I was reluctant to turn on a light. The archbishop was in the building, and no excuse would be reasonable for invading his office at this hour. But I needed information, and I needed the light to find it. I closed the door, felt for the lamp on a table near the wall, and turned it on.

Four file cabinets sat side-by-side against a wall. The archbishop's mistrust of computer technology made him keep hard copies of everything.

Where to begin?

I knew that the first and second cabinet contained files on parishes in the diocese—financial documents, parish anniversary brochures, pastoral reports. The third cabinet contained diocesan financial information.

Whatever information existed on Jack would be in the fourth cabinet. I approached it, hesitating before trying the top drawer. Did I really want to find information on Jack's past? What if it ruined everything we had?

But I'd gone too far now to turn back. Whatever was plaguing Jack seemed beyond his control, and maybe beyond his ability to communicate it.

I proceeded to open the drawer, but it was locked. So were the others.

Odds were high that the key was in one of the desk drawers.

Knowing himself to be absentminded, the archbishop kept everything he needed within easy reach.

In the back of the middle drawer, I found a ring with four small keys—probably for each of the cabinets. I returned to the fourth one and started trying the keys. Finally, one worked.

In the top drawer I found files full of letters. Some were complaints from parishioners. Others were very personal letters from priests. I tried not to look at the names of the writers. *Keep focused,* I told myself.

The second drawer contained more such letters, and then a file marked *Confidential.* As I slipped it out of the drawer, several letters fell out.

"Shit," I blurted. What if the letters had been in some kind of order?

When I crouched to recover them, I thought I heard a noise in the hallway. I froze, glancing at the lamp, all the way across the room. But it was better to leave it on. The darkness would cast suspicion on me if it was the archbishop.

I waited for the door to open. But nothing happened. There was no more noise. I figured I'd been wrong. No one was in the hallway. Relieved, I opened several letters. All were formal evaluations of priests in alcohol recovery programs. Corey's name appeared several times.

In the next drawer I came across a file labeled *Father John R. Canston.* I carried it to the desk and thumbed through the papers. They were mostly letters of recommendation from the bishop of Montana and parish board members, as well as application documents for transferring to the diocese. I scanned the letters for evidence of problems, but they were all filled with glowing terms: "a truly committed priest"; "inspirational piety"; "revived the dying parish within three years." In the back of the file was a manila envelope. The return address was that of the state hospital of Montana—mental health division. I unfastened the envelope's metal clasp. There was nothing inside.

I searched each file drawer for the missing contents, whatever they were, but I found nothing with hospital letterhead. Then I searched the desk drawers without success.

I was ready to admit defeat, when a knock at the door startled me. An announcement followed. "It's Jack, Archbishop. Everything okay?"

I laid the envelope face down over Jack's file and opened the door.

"What are you doing?" Jack said, surprised. He was in jeans and a sweatshirt now.

"The archbishop wanted me to work on a report. I couldn't sleep, so I figured I might as well do something."

"A report?"

"Financial stuff on St. John's. For the diocese."

Jack glanced beyond me at the desk. "I'm sorry. I've been an asshole."

"No." I touched his arm. "I'm the one who's been an asshole. I'm trying to move everything too fast."

"Let's go back to bed."

"I'll be up in a minute," I said. "After I put this stuff back." I nodded to the desk.

When Jack left, I replaced everything and locked the door. I felt strangely reluctant to join Jack. I wasn't sure if it was because of shame or apprehension.

Jack Canston's Journal

January 12

I fucking lost it when I saw the dog. When will it end? Those faces? Those voices?

Gotta keep it together—if not for me, then for my sheep. And Danny needs solid direction. Souls are at stake. Come on, Canston, get it together!

I pray to you, God. Do you hear me? *Incline your ear, O Lord, and answer me, for I am poor and needy. Preserve my life, for I am devoted to you.*

The electricians started wiring the rectory today. It won't be long, I'll have a place to go away from St. John's. I thought being here would help. I thought the old memories would wash everything away. But the place is messing with my mind. It's making me need *him*. He's making everything get muddled together. If I can't keep things in their place, what good will I be as a priest?

Holy Mary, Mother of God, pray for me!

7

ON SATURDAY MORNING I got a strange call from Mrs. Flores, Danny's mother. She was very upset and said she had to tell me something in person. When I suggested that she talk to Jack instead of me, since he was her pastor, she responded with alarm.

"No, no, Father! He can't know. Please don't tell him I talked to you."

I figured she was embarrassed by her problem and needed to confide in a priest who wouldn't be looking her in the eye every Sunday morning as he served her communion.

"All right," I agreed. "Why don't you come by my office on Monday?"

"It can't wait, Father! I have to tell you today. And I can only get away from the restaurant for an hour or so between lunch and dinner. Could you come to my house?"

The last thing I wanted was to spend my Saturday afternoon on the interstate, and I hesitated.

"Please, Father," she begged. "It's very important."

At three o'clock, I pulled up in front of the Floreses' little house. It was just a block from the family restaurant in the Mexican neighborhood that had grown up around Santa Rosa's. The vinyl siding was clean and white. The concrete porch was painted battleship gray. In front of it, a plaster figure of the Virgin Mary extended her arms over the tiny front yard, patchy with snow.

Mrs. Flores came to the door before I rang the bell. She wore a stained white sweatshirt with her restaurant's name swirled in red letters, *La Sorpresa.* The feathery style of her short, raven hair flattered her round face and large, gentle eyes. She greeted me anxiously and led me into the house.

Chairs and a couch in floral upholstery crowded the paneled living room. On the television, votive candles clustered around a framed photograph of the Virgin of Guadalupe depicted in the church. The house smelled of fried onions.

"Please have a seat, Father." She gestured to a recliner and took a seat herself on the sofa, perching on the edge.

"What's on your mind, Mrs. Flores?"

She chewed on her lip and nervously turned the wedding band on her finger. I hadn't noticed the ring before. At the funeral she'd mentioned that she was a single mother. I assumed now that she was a widow.

"It's all right," I said. "Take your time."

"Oh, Father," she blurted. "It's horrible." She glanced at the photo of the Virgin on the television. "It's Danny. And Father Jack."

"What about them?"

She lowered her eyes to her white sneakers, chewing her lip some more and twisting the ring. Then she brought her plump hand to her chest as though she was trying to calm herself. Finally, she looked at me. "Yesterday afternoon, Danny told me he had an appointment with Father Jack at the church. For spiritual direction. Fridays are busy at the restaurant, so I don't like him to take off on Fridays. But he's been through so much trouble. And now he's so good—going to church, praying. He loves the Blessed Virgin! So of course I let him go." She stopped. She covered her mouth with her hand and started to cry.

"It's all right, Mrs. Flores," I managed to say, full of dread. "It's all right."

She pulled a tissue from the box on the end table, and wiped her nose. "I was starting to make the ceviche," she continued. "And I realized I'd left the shrimp at home in the fridge. Danny has a cell phone, but I didn't want to bother him during his spiritual counseling, so I just ran home myself. When I got here, Father Jack's truck was parked in front of the house. I thought they must have come here to talk. I didn't want to bother them, so I came in the back door, quietly. I looked down the hallway and noticed the living room lights were off. Danny's bedroom door was partly closed, but the light wasn't on and I didn't hear any voices. So I pushed open the door."

I already knew what she had seen, and I didn't want to hear the words. My chest tightened so much, I could barely breathe.

"They were in bed, Father," she whispered, choking up. "They weren't wearing anything. I just stood there and stared. Danny yelled at me to get out."

I watched her sob, too shocked and angry to feel anything for her.

When she finally got hold of herself, she looked at me desperately. "I'm worried about Danny's soul. If something happens to him, he'll go straight to hell. To do something so evil. And with a holy priest. To ruin a priest!"

"Father Jack is the one responsible," I said. "Not Danny."

The point didn't seem to register in her mind. "Can you stop it?" she pleaded. "Can you talk to Danny? Tell him how much his soul is in danger?"

"I'll talk to Father Jack."

"No, please! Don't tell him I told you. He's our pastor."

"That's right," I said. "And you did the right thing to tell me about this. Don't worry about Father Jack. He won't blame you."

The words didn't appear to reassure her. But she seemed resigned to my decision.

She poured out her soul for a while longer, though I was so upset that I hardly heard a thing that she said. Before I left, she asked me to bless Danny's room, as if I could purge the evil that now contaminated it. I don't know why I agreed to do it, but I did. As I stood in the dark, cramped room, I imagined Jack and Danny entangled on the bed.

It was almost four, and I knew that Jack was at Santa Rosa's preparing for the Saturday evening mass, so I drove to the church, pulling up next to his pickup in the parking lot.

Jack's voice boomed at me over the sound system as I entered the vestibule. I could see him through the doorway. Dressed in his clerical shirt and Roman collar, he stood in the pulpit, rehearsing his sermon. The starry blue sky of the mosaic loomed behind him on the wall of the apse, with Juan Diego in the center, in adoration before the holy Virgin. The pews were empty.

Jack nodded at me as I approached him but kept preaching. "And what does the Gospel say? Anyone who wants to be my disciple must deny his very self, pick up his cross, and follow me. Whoever would save his life will lose it. Whoever will lose it for my sake will save it. So we've got to stop worrying about self-preservation. Because self-preservation isn't living. Risk-taking is."

I stopped directly in front of the pulpit and interrupted him. "Risk-taking?" I said. "What a joke!"

"What's wrong?" Jack turned off the microphone and gazed down at me suspiciously, like he knew why I was furious.

"I just talked to Danny's mother."

"Chris . . ." he started to explain, then glanced around to make sure no one was there.

"I want everyone to know!" I shouted. "They should know just how much they can trust Father Jack!"

Jack clambered down from the pulpit and grabbed my arm. "Let's talk in the sacristy."

I pulled away from him. "How could you do this?"

"It only happened once."

I shook my head, thinking how stupid I'd been for trying to dismiss Danny's infatuation. "You want him?" I asked ruefully. "You can have him."

The front door suddenly banged, and voices echoed in the vestibule. Two old women hobbled into the church, dipping their hands into the fonts on either side of the doorway and blessing themselves. I stared at Jack, a flood of emotion rushing violently through me. How could he do this? Why had I ever hoped for anything from someone who made up his own rules about church and God and sex? It was over between us. Forever. As if there had ever been anything between us to begin with!

I pulled away from him, my eyes hot with tears, and headed up the aisle and past the women.

He followed me. I heard one of the women ask him to bless her new rosary, but I didn't hear him respond. As I reached the front door he called after me.

I turned back to him, full of betrayal and loss. "It's over," I said.

He looked panic-stricken, his face as white as milk. But he didn't try to stop me again.

Part Two

THE REVERSAL

O afflicted one, storm-battered and unconsoled,
I lay your pavements in carnelians,
and your foundations in sapphires;
I will make your battlements of rubies,
your gates of carbuncles,
and all your walls of precious stones.

—ISAIAH 54.11–13

8

IN THE DAYS that followed the breakup, my mood vacillated between rage and desolation. The rage was easier to take, and so I cultivated it, replaying the moments over the past weeks when I'd suspected something between Jack and Danny. I imagined them laughing at me behind my back. And I imagined confronting Jack for betraying me. While I jogged, I actually blathered aloud hatefully at him, like a schizophrenic.

In my anger at Jack, I thought a lot about Eddie, because he had always hated Jack for the awe he inspired. And the more I had worshipped Jack during our high school days, the more I had treated Eddie like dirt. Now I felt sorrier than ever, and I saw Eddie as my ally. I took comfort in my memories of him.

I remembered vividly the day Eddie and I met. In my assigned alcove in the large, open dorm, I was unpacking clothes on my bed when Eddie marched up to me. Blackheads sprouted all over his face.

He wore a short-sleeved shirt with black and white and yellow vertical stripes, and white pants. He had an old-fashioned haircut, with the sides of his head buzzed and the top oiled and parted down the middle. The haircut and his round glasses made him look like he'd stepped out of a barber shop quartet.

"I'm Edward Joseph Gerhardt," he'd announced with a feminine lilt in his voice. He stuck out his hand, holding it close to his chest, all the long fingers together.

When I tried to shake it, he pulled it away and wiggled it around like a snake.

His eyes gleamed with satisfaction. "Not fast enough," he said, shaking his finger at me. I noticed a Mickey Mouse watch on his wrist.

"Guess what my favorite TV show is." He watched me slyly as I fumbled for an answer, taken aback by the abrupt question and by him in general.

"I don't know? *Little House on the Prairie*?" My intuition said he'd like something traditional.

He thought about it, as though he hadn't considered that answer but should have. Then he shook his head and gave me the right answer, *The Lawrence Welk Show.*

He threw up his hands as though he held an imaginary dance partner and began waltzing around the linoleum, singing, "Good night. Sleep tight. And pleasant dreams to you." That was the first time I noticed his red plaid slippers.

He waltzed around the four beds in my bay and then vanished down the hall, crooning the good-night song to other newcomers.

That night as I and my three bay-mates got ready for bed, Eddie waltzed by again in pajamas blotched like a cow, serenading us with the Lawrence Welk tune. It was a ritual he religiously observed all of freshman year.

By the time Jack arrived at St. John's the next year, Eddie and I had become fast friends, sneaking down to the recreation rooms at night to watch horror movies, working out clarinet and piano duets, running through our lines together for class plays—Eddie frequently in the wig and dress of a female character he'd volunteered to play.

Safe behind the walls of St. John's, I wasn't worried about being associated with such an effeminate boy. But all that changed when Jack arrived. I was immediately in awe of this sober, confident, handsome stranger. I wasn't alone. My class soon elected him president, and the junior varsity cross-country team made him captain.

When I started reciting the rosary with him, I was impressed by his disciplined, intelligent piety—worlds apart from Eddie's fussy, scrupulous kind, which inspired his plastic flowers arranged around saints' pictures. Jack's was a distinctly masculine brand—the kind that inspired jocks to pray. Everything about Jack was masculine. And I longed for his masculinity.

So Eddie went by the wayside. As I became more sober, under Jack's influence, Eddie became less and less amusing. I avoided him and judged him. And he finally called me on it.

It was on an autumn night. Eddie woke me up and ordered me to watch an old King Kong movie with him. In the security lights I could make out a bag of potato chips and a can of soda in his hands. When I told him to get lost, he poured the drink on my face and dropped the can. I jumped out of bed and chased him around the enclosed central area of the dorm, where the toilets and showers were. All the while, he kept shrieking, "You beast! You beast!"

Kids woke up and yelled at us to cut it out. Afraid to be caught with Eddie by Jack, I stopped, maturely returned to my bed, and started changing the wet sheets. As long as I lived, I'd never forget the look of bitter betrayal on Eddie's face when he reappeared in my bay in his cow pajamas and plaid slippers, still clutching his potato chips.

"You used to be fun, Seib," he said. "Before you became Canston's slave."

Jack was awake by then. He ordered Eddie to go back to bed.

Eddie flipped him off with his long middle finger. He dropped the chips and pranced away.

After that, he snubbed me, spitting out a hateful comment every once in a while, but never causing another scene.

Secretly, I'd always known that Eddie was right to reproach me. I really had turned myself into Jack's slave. For Jack, I probably would have agreed to self-immolation in the name of Christ. But at least back then I'd had the excuse of youth. Now, I asked myself, what had been my excuse for submitting to Jack again? For living in his fantasy world where we could be priests and lovers, despite the cold dictates of the church?

I was resolved. I wouldn't let myself be seduced again. I knelt in the chapel one night—in the pew where Jack and I had knelt together a thousand times—and made a vow to God: no more lies. Christ help me!

THE FOLLOWING SUNDAY I substituted for a sick priest in a wealthy Lawrence parish. The new church included a grade school and an enormous family center with a fellowship hall and a gym. Framed photos of the pope abounded on the walls. The tall, lanky president of the parish council beamed as he guided me through the facilities.

After saying three masses packed with young parents and noisy kids, I was exhausted. I waited at a large picture window in the rectory for Jack's pickup to pull into the drive. My car was in the shop, and after almost a week of avoiding Jack—despite his overtures—I asked him to pick me up. The silent treatment couldn't go on forever, and I wanted to give him back the toiletries he kept in my bathroom.

The pickup finally pulled into the driveway, a rosary dangling from the rearview mirror. Tense, but determined to normalize our relationship, I climbed in. Jack looked haggard. He hadn't shaved. I felt such tenderness for him, I was afraid I'd kiss him.

"What's this?" I said, pointing to his cheek but forcing myself not to touch it. "You growing a beard?"

Jack shrugged without answering. He lit a cigarette and cracked the window. Then he pulled out of the driveway and headed down the street past expensive new Tudor-style homes. "Protestors showed up at Santa Rosa's," he said. "They flashed big signs at people as they entered the church. 'God hates fags.' Really nice. The same group showed up at St. Pat's and Our Lady of Sorrows. They're making the rounds at all the parishes."

Everyone in Topeka was all too familiar with the homophobic group started by a self-proclaimed evangelical minister with a mission to stamp out homosexuality. The group frequently appeared with signs in front of local businesses rumored to have gay employees and at nearly every church they deemed too liberal. Apparently they weren't satisfied with the Vatican's recent mandate against ordaining gay men. They wanted the Catholic Church to ban homosexuals from even entering the doors of a church.

"That's too bad," I said, without sympathy. I felt secretly vindicated, despite my disgust at the protestors. Jack deserved to be punished.

Jack cast me a wounded glance. "You don't give a damn. Do you?"

I shrugged without responding.

We stopped at the turnpike booth on the interstate, and Jack accepted a ticket from the bearded attendant. For a while we rode quietly along the highway, the drab countryside now visible under splotches of snow, bright in the sunshine.

"It really was just once, Chris," he finally said, imploringly. He stubbed out his cigarette and turned to me. "It was a horrible mistake. My nerves were frayed. I gave in. But it's never happened again."

"It doesn't matter."

"So can we go back to the way we were?" His eyes pleaded with me, their golden flecks glimmering in soft brown irises.

I shook my head. "I can't live like that."

"But if it's a matter of trust—"

"It's not just that," I interrupted. "It's sneaking around. Pretending. Never getting to celebrate our anniversaries with friends."

Jack planted his square hand on my leg. "I need you."

I could see how much it cost him to bare his soul like this. It took every ounce of willpower I had not to clutch his hand and give in to the voice inside of me shouting, *He needs* you *now. It's not a matter of submitting.* But then I reminded myself that Jack's way *did* mean submission—if not to him, then to the old order of things.

"You already have me," I finally said, moving his hand from my leg. "As a friend."

He nodded with bitter resignation and gazed forlornly at the road, barely speaking for the rest of the drive. I didn't try to reassure him. How could I?

When we got back to St. John's, we parked in the underground garage and took the elevator up to our floor. Jack looked so sullen, I figured he'd want to get away from me. But when we reached his door, he took me by the arm.

"Would you at least come in and have a drink?"

I thought this was his way of taking the high road, letting bygones be bygones. Still, I couldn't be sure. And I didn't want to test my power of resistance.

"Please," he whispered. "I want to tell you something."

It occurred to me that maybe now he was desperate enough to break down and reveal his hospitalization. Maybe he thought that would win me back. Whatever his motives, I told myself, if I really did plan to be his friend I had to listen. So I followed him in.

The living room was a wreck. Dirty plates cluttered the coffee table. Full ashtrays sat on the desk and the end tables, next to empty beer bottles. Several thick theology books lay open on the carpet, as though they'd been thrown there. I noticed that one was a commentary on Aquinas's *Summa Theologica*. Pages evidently torn from the books also littered the floor. I could see his bed was unmade in the other room, and clothes were heaped on the floor. The closed rooms smelled funky, almost feral, combining the odors of soiled clothing, tobacco, and dried food.

"I've just been a little crazy," he said, by way of explanation as I gazed around the room. "Here. Sit down."

He cleared some clothes from the couch, and I took a seat. He grabbed a couple of dirty glasses from the desk, rinsed them in the bathroom, and poured us some bourbon from a bottle on the bookshelf.

He seemed to make a point of sitting on the opposite end of the couch to show he took my words seriously. "To friendship," he said, lifting his glass.

I raised mine and we both drank. In a second gulp, he finished all his bourbon and plopped the glass on one of the dirty plates. "Jesus. It's hot in here," he said, tugging at his sweater. He pulled it over his head and slipped the little white tab from his clerical shirt and undid the top two buttons, exposing the dark hair that crept up to his throat.

The heat was turned up high in the room, and I was pretty warm myself. But I didn't want to send the wrong signal, so I left my sweater on.

"What did you want to tell me?" I said.

He rubbed his cheek in the agitated way I'd seen him do on the night we found the dog. Then he scooted closer to me. "Look, Chris, I'm serious. I need you. Just look around this room. Can you see I've been going crazy? If you want me to beg you, I will." He ventured closer. I could smell the liquor on his breath.

His heavy beard and his oily hair, ruffled from his sweater, heightened the strangely sleazy sensuality he exuded. Combined with the desperation in his eyes, it made him irresistible. He grabbed my glass and set it on the table. Then he fell on my neck like some kind of wild animal determined to feed on me, yanking down the sweater to get to my bare skin. I couldn't resist him. I let him yank off the sweater and rip open my shirt, popping the buttons. He lifted my legs onto the couch, straddled me, and pinned back my arms to nuzzle my bare chest. As he worked his way down my belly, releasing my arms, I tried to force myself to shove him off. But I couldn't do it. I was hot with excitement.

He tore open his pants, and his purple erection bobbed up. But when he brought it to my mouth as if to feed me, a voice inside of me seemed to scream, "No. Don't!" Then I realized I'd actually said the words.

"Just suck it," Jack pleaded, trying to force himself between my lips.

I tried to push him away, but he grabbed my head and pulled it to his dick. The delicious, musky smell of his crotch almost made me open, but I didn't. When Jack saw I wouldn't, he released me and stood up.

"I'm sorry," he said, still beautifully erect, clearly distraught.

"No you're not." Mad at myself, mad at him, I grabbed my clothes and left, glancing back wistfully at his bare ass.

IN THE MORNING I found a note on the floor just inside the living room door. Jack's printed message was to the point: *Please take me back. I'll die without you. Just tell me what you want, and I'll do it.*

I knew in my gut this was a promise he couldn't keep, because my only demand would be for him to leave the priesthood with me. And how could I extract a promise like this from him when he was in this desperate state? Especially when I didn't know what I really wanted myself. Was I really ready to give up the only world I knew? Even if I was, where would I go, and how would I make a living? I wadded up the note and threw it away.

An hour later as I sat in my office, Jack called me.

"Did you get the note?" he said.

"It won't work, Jack. We want different things." I forced these words out, my gaze focused on the contemporary print of Christ above the sofa. In it a rugged, Middle Eastern–looking Jesus sat cross-legged on a mountainside, surrounded by men and women, and he was laughing a big, toothy laugh. At the moment, he seemed to be laughing at me.

"Everything was perfect before," Jack continued. "Please, Chris. I'm going crazy."

"What's the matter with you, Jack? That night we found the dog—" Before I could get out another word, he hung up.

The phone rang again in five minutes, but I didn't answer it. I knew it was Jack. What was the use talking again? I was already shaken, and I had work to do. I decided not to answer the phone for the rest of the day and just periodically play my messages. Over the course of the day, Jack left three messages. I didn't listen to them. As soon as I heard his voice, I hit the delete button.

That evening I went to a movie with Alberta to avoid him. I thought it would distract me, too, but no such luck. My mind was on him through the whole film. When I got back, I stood outside his door, longing to go in to him. But somehow I moved on to my apartment.

The next day there were no calls. I was half relieved and half disappointed. By the end of the day, I decided to call him. When I did, he didn't answer. Then I remembered that he spent Wednesdays visiting homebound parishioners. They'd probably kept him distracted. And on Wednesday evenings he taught a Bible class at the parish. I figured I'd swim some hard laps and go to bed early.

But after laps that night, I found myself constantly at the window, waiting for his truck to circle around to the parking garage. When it finally appeared, I turned out the lights and got into bed. If he thought I was asleep, he wouldn't knock, and I wouldn't have to push him away. But five minutes later, when the knock came anyway, I felt relieved. I got up and opened the door.

Jack stood there in his coat, weary-eyed. "I'm ready to be friends," he said.

"All right," I responded, despite my doubts.

"Tomorrow night, let's rent a movie. And we'll just watch it. Nothing else."

"I don't know, Jack. Maybe we should take a break from each other for a little while."

That strange look of agitation came over him. "Look, I'm trying, Chris. Give me a break."

I couldn't stand seeing him like this. "Okay."

Without another word, he walked away.

IN THE MORNING, I met with a woman from Jack's parish to arrange a group retreat at St. John's. We talked in my office and then went over to inspect the dormitory where her people would be staying.

"How many in your group, Mrs. Navarro?" I followed the dark-haired woman into a dormitory room. The old bays in the underclass dorm had now been enclosed, forming twelve spacious rooms, each furnished with four single beds, a desk, and two upholstered armchairs.

"There should be thirty or forty." She touched a crucifix on the wall and made the sign of the cross. "Unless my novena to the Blessed Mother works. Then we'll have a dozen more."

I nodded, adding the information to the form I carried on a clipboard. As usual, my mind was on Jack. As if she could read my thoughts, Mrs. Navarro suddenly brought him up.

"I'm so happy that Father Jack agreed to lead the Cursillo," she said. "Our group at Santa Rosa's prayed that the new pastor would be devoted to the Blessed Mother and lead our Cursillos. Our prayers came true."

Her brown eyes glowed. She was the picture of health, her complexion smooth, her teeth straight and bright. Her red turtleneck sweater accentuated her full bosom. She had told me that her spirituality group at Santa Rosa's also observed a diet and exercise program. "We need healthy bodies to serve our Lord," she'd added, beaming.

"Now, in terms of using the chapel . . ." I said.

"Oh, we want perpetual adoration. During Cursillos the Blessed Sacrament stays exposed on the altar. There's an around-the-clock vigil. Everyone signs up for several hours a day. Except during mass, of course."

Cookie worship. I scribbled to hide my annoyance. Of course, Eucharistic Adoration, as it was officially called, had been a harmless Catholic tradition for centuries. But in the intense spiritual experience aimed at in Cursillo retreats, it reached the point of fanaticism. "You know, Mrs. Navarro, we've never had a Cursillo at St. John's. Why don't you tell me what to expect?"

As we headed to my office, Mrs. Navarro gushed about the intense retreat created by a spiritual renewal movement originating in Spain. It included praying in tongues, singing in Spanish, all-night vigils in adoration, rosaries, and ample opportunities for confession.

"Will you be available for confession, too, Father? One priest is not enough. Lots of people in our group like to go to confession every day."

I cringed at the thought of sitting in the confessional, a captive audience for housewives eaten away by guilt for not submitting to their husbands. *Hell no!* I wanted to shout. But what could I say—I'm a priest but I don't do confessions, at least not for people with a martyr complex? I finally relented and told her I'd help out.

In my office, I finished filling out the form and accepted a deposit check from Mrs. Navarro. I got up when she stood to put on her coat.

"I'm on my way to the abortion clinic in Topeka," she said. "Our group goes once a week to protest. Here, Father. We all wear this." She handed me a little gold pin shaped like two feet. "It symbolizes the unborn babies. Have a nice day."

As soon as Mrs. Navarro left, Debbie Cook, my secretary, appeared at the door. She was a sweet woman in her fifties with a mass of auburn hair and a chronically flushed face. Her glasses dangled from a chain around her neck.

"There are two young men to see you, Father. They don't have an appointment. Is that all right?"

"Sure, Debbie. Send them in."

I got up to greet the visitors when they appeared at the door. They introduced themselves as Mark and Barry. Both were tall, good-looking kids. Mark had a shaved head, a heavy beard, and a stud in his nose. Barry was slender and suave, with large, aquiline features. I invited them to sit down on the sofa and took a seat in one of the two club chairs facing them. They unzipped their matching leather jackets.

"What can I do for you guys?"

"We want to get married," Mark said, in a loud, baritone voice. He sounded like a truck driver from New Jersey.

"You mean the two of you?" I waved my finger at them.

Mark nodded. "And we want to do it right. Caterer, photographer, priest—the whole nine yards. We love the chapel here." He took hold of Barry's hand.

"We're in this for life," Barry said, proudly.

"Are you both Catholic?" I couldn't believe they were so clueless about church teaching.

"Hey, I was confirmed," Mark said. "But the folks weren't much on church."

"My family is a bunch of pagans," Barry chuckled. "But I think it's important for us to belong to a church. We're thinking about adopting a kid—from Russia. Some friends of ours just did. We want to be good, church-going parents." He smiled a beautiful smile at Mark.

I was touched by their naïveté, but I had to bring them back to earth. "You know, the Catholic Church doesn't allow gay weddings."

"Not officially," Barry said, casting Mark a knowing glance.

Puzzled, I asked him what he meant.

"Father Corey said that priests can perform the ceremony sort of under the table."

"Father Corey Mulhane?" I asked, starting to understand.

"He said you'd be cool about letting us use St. John's chapel," Mark chimed in, confidently. "He'll officiate, if that's okay."

Searching for a way to disabuse them of their fantasy, I studied the print of the smiling Christ. *Fucking Mulhane.* I wanted to strangle him. Of course, I *could* actually do it. Plan the wedding for a weekend when the archbishop was out of town. Flout the rules. Let Koch defrock me when he found out.

But I didn't have the balls. As my rebellious fantasy evaporated, my gaze finally moved from the picture on the wall to the pair on the sofa, looking expectantly at me. "Father Mulhane is wrong," I said. "A gay wedding would be grounds for kicking me out of the priesthood."

"You're fucking kidding!" Mark said. "Jesus, it's not like it's legal or anything."

"Father Corey seemed really cool about it," Barry said, perplexed.

I leaned forward and said something I never dreamed I would say. The words just seemed to pour out on their own. "My advice—find a church where you can be yourself."

"Like where?" Mark said.

I shrugged. "I don't have a clue."

They seemed disappointed, but they said they'd do some research to find a church that would welcome them with open arms—if one existed. They thanked me for my help. I suppose they appreciated my honesty. They must have sensed my own frustration with my church. Mark eyed me sympathetically and asked, "Why do you put up with it?"

"As a gay man," I said, "I sure as hell don't know."

They didn't seem at all surprised by the admission.

As they got up to leave, Mark turned to me and patted my back. "When we find a good church, we'll give you a call."

I smiled. "Thanks."

After they'd gone, I sat at my desk, reflectively fingering the little gold pin Mrs. Navarro had left with me. The two morning interviews dramatized my options. I could either remain venerated but stifled in an oppressive institution, or I could be free and give up everything that had ever given my life meaning—and security.

Then I reminded myself that leaving the priesthood meant leaving what linked me to Jack. And I imagined Jack whispering in my ear, "Priesthood is the life you were called to. Stay, and have it all!" And after all these years of dedication, didn't I deserve it all?

Yes, I did. I sighed and tossed the little pin into the trash. Then I sat down and sent Corey a nasty e-mail for his little prank.

AT SEVEN THAT evening, Jack showed up at my apartment with a pizza and a video. He looked much better. His jeans and gray sweatshirt looked clean. He'd shaved and washed his hair. He looked rested, too. I was happy to see him this way. Maybe it meant he'd accepted the change in our relationship, and now I could, too.

"What's the movie?"

He handed it to me and deposited the pizza on the coffee table.

I almost groaned when I saw the title: *Song of Bernadette.* The saccharine film about Lourdes was the last thing I wanted to watch. But I figured Jack had his reasons for choosing it, and I didn't want to ruin the evening by complaining.

Jack seemed to read my thoughts. "It's a tribute to Eddie," he gently explained. He was sincere. He wasn't judging Eddie for his mortal sin.

He popped the video into the VCR. I opened a couple of the beers

I'd retrieved from the staff kitchen. And we both sat on the couch, our feet on the coffee table, pizza in our laps, watching the film.

Jack was silent during the movie. When I glanced at him from time to time, I could see his attention was riveted on it. He didn't even distract himself long enough to light a cigarette during the film. He just sat with his arms folded, a look of reverent longing on his face, as though he would will himself into the scenes if he could. At one point, when little Bernadette rubbed mud on her face as directed by the Virgin Mary, Jack's eyes filled with tears.

I wanted more than anything to throw my arms around him and ask him again to tell me the reason for his awful sorrow, but I knew it was no use.

When the movie was over, he said a quick good-bye and promptly left. He seemed determined to prove to me that I wouldn't have to fight him off whenever we spent time together. I told myself I should be relieved, but my apartment felt like the loneliest place in the world without him.

For the next couple of days, he didn't call me at all, and I only saw him once, briefly in the hallway. He looked preoccupied but determined to keep his promise. The distance was harder for me to take than his pleading. I wondered if he thought playing hard to get would make me run to him. The fact is, it almost did. I couldn't stand it. I hated not sleeping with him, not touching him.

Then on Friday, when I hoped we could spend the evening together, Danny showed up. I saw Jack and him praying in the chapel. Then I heard them go into Jack's apartment. I actually listened at the door. When I couldn't hear anything, I imagined the worst. I wanted to rush in. But I returned to my apartment and tried to read. Still unable to concentrate after an hour, I returned to Jack's door. Again I heard nothing. Either they were sitting quietly in the living room, or they were in the bedroom. And if they were in the bedroom . . . I hated the images that flashed before my eyes of their naked bodies wrestling on the bed. I figured that since I'd rebuffed Jack, he saw no reason to renounce his desire for Danny. Or maybe he was purposefully trying to hurt me. Maybe his new restraint signaled a turn in his mind. Maybe he'd turned cold-blooded and mean.

Now I was the desperate one. I could stay there and go crazy with jealousy or get out of the building and break Jack's hold on me.

Like a junkie needing a fix, I grabbed my coat and keys, rushed down to my car, and sped off toward downtown Kansas City. When the skyline of bright skyscrapers loomed ahead of me, I turned up the radio to shut out the moralizing voices at the edges of my thoughts. I exited in the warehouse district and drove under the viaduct past gloomy, boarded-up buildings. Dirty snow plowed from the street formed mounds along the curb.

A neon sign on a warehouse flashed the word "Rendez-Vous." I'd seen the bar advertised in a gay newspaper I'd picked up in a Starbucks one morning. I pulled into the parking lot, which held a dozen cars. I didn't know much about gay bars—I'd only been in a couple during my college days, but I knew it was still early for dancing. According to the ad, however, the place had a restaurant, and I could wait there for the crowds to arrive.

Inside the dark foyer, I followed the signs to a restaurant in a loft above the dance floor. Several couples were dining, as well as a large group of rowdy biker types. The tall, bald host led me to a table. A slender waiter with bleached blond hair brought me a cocktail, then two more before I decided to eat something. While I was reading the menu, a guy with a goatee sat down at the bar. He ordered a drink and gazed at me unabashedly. I eyed him back and he sauntered over to my table, a bottle of beer in hand.

"You want some company?" he said. He was a freckled redhead in a Broncos football jersey. Up close I could see he wasn't as young as I'd first thought. His forehead was lined, and he had crow's feet around his beautiful blue eyes. He must have been thirty-five or so.

"Sure."

He sat down and ordered another beer and a hamburger.

"I'm Scotty." He shook my hand. "I've never seen you here before."

"It's my first time here."

"Really? Did you just move to the area? This is the oldest bar in the city."

"I don't get out much."

Scotty laughed and patted my hand.

For the next hour and a half he chattered about his job at a local Kinko's and about his recent breakup with a guy from Chicago who stole cash and CDs from him. By then I regretted coming to the bar, but Scotty was there for the taking, and Jack was with his handsome protégé.

When we finished eating, I followed Scotty back to his garden apartment across from a gas station. The living room held a futon, a recliner, and a console with a television and stereo. On the wall hung a huge framed poster of Marilyn Monroe in the famous dress-blowing scene.

Scotty suddenly dropped to his knees, unfastened my pants, and took me into his mouth. *It's for your own good,* I told myself, staring at Marilyn's flying skirts. And I let him bring me the comfort I needed.

Jack Canston's Journal

January 21

"God has bestowed man with reason to govern his passions." Bullshit! What did fat Thomas Aquinas know about it? What do any of the fucking theologians know about it? Have they ever had a drum beating inside their head, counting off the final minutes before the nightmare rushes back and seizes them? Have they ever loved a man so much they thought they'd die without him? I never have—not until now. And he's gone. The only one I've ever wanted. Gone because of my weak flesh.

I almost told David the truth when he called and said, "What's going on, bro? Are you losing it again? Are you on the meds? Dad said to ask you because you're bullheaded." I asked him if he thought I'd still be alive and talking to him if I wasn't on the meds. He said, "If you ever wanna talk about it, man, I'm here." Bullshit. He doesn't want to talk about it, and he knows I don't or he wouldn't ask me. I'll never talk about it. If I do, they win, not me. If I do, I'll be no good as a priest.

Today I baptized a baby. It was so innocent I wanted to cry. And I wanted to squeeze the life out of it. God help me!

9

ON SUNDAY AFTERNOON, I sat in the St. John's chapel among fifty priests gathered in the section of pews facing the altar. The archbishop had called a special meeting to address the Vatican's new policy against homosexuals in the priesthood. I'd almost refused to attend. Then I decided I needed to hear what he had to say. I needed to know where the likes of me stood in this grand fraternity.

There was no sign of Jack yet. Maybe he wouldn't show up. In his state, the last thing he needed was to hear this kind of crap—no matter how good he was at shutting it out.

After last night's tryst, I felt foolish for my desperation. Jealousy and paranoia had gotten the best of me. I had no reason to believe Jack was still sleeping with Danny. In fact, I'd seen Danny leaving the dorm on the morning after my little adventure. He'd evidently spent the night there, alone.

The archbishop finally entered the chapel, genuflected, and turned to face us, the altar looming behind him on the slate platform. He looked tired and defeated, ready to pour out his soul. He touched his pectoral cross through his black jacket, as though to draw strength from it.

"We've experienced a devastating tragedy recently," he began, his weak voice straining to be heard. "One of our brothers has been violently wrenched from us. God knows what Father Edward went through. And what his family has gone through. We have suffered, too. Not only for the loss of a brother, but for our own deep wound. When one of us takes his own life, all that we stand for is called into question."

Heads nodded in agreement.

The archbishop continued. "I know that rumors have been spreading about what led Father Edward to do this horrible thing. Apparently someone painted a foul accusation on the side of the garage at St. Mary's where Edward took his own life, and several people in the congregation have called me about painful gossip circulating. Whether the rumors are true or not, the scandal caused even by such a possibility damages the church's credibility. That is why the new Vatican mandate is so important. The mandate is an effort to purge the clergy of sexual deviants. The church has always taught that homosexuality is an intrinsically disordered condition. We may have compassion on homosexuals, but it would be a mistake to allow them to function as spiritual leaders in the church."

Monsignior Spiegel, a gray-haired priest with bushy eyebrows and heavy jowls, raised his hand.

"Yes, Monsignior?" the archbishop said.

The old priest stood. "I respectfully disagree, Archbishop. Everyone knows that the priesthood has always attracted so-called sexual deviants. And why not? Since the church has ordered them to be celibate anyway, why not be celibate as priests?"

I wanted to stand up and cheer for old Spiegel, as stodgy as they come but ready to stand up for the truth. The archbishop was frowning, but the troublemaker continued.

"My forty years in the priesthood tell me that at least a quarter of my brothers are homosexual—maybe the number is much larger. Many of these men have been excellent priests. They've struggled with celibacy no more and no less than heterosexual priests. How can the church turn its back on its sons? They've served the church well. Many have been excellent musicians and artists." He raised his hand as though to forestall a protest—as unlikely as hell in that group of fuddy-duddies. "I realize this is a stereotype, but there's some truth to the special sensibilities of so-called deviants. The church owes some of its greatest, most moving musical compositions to such men." Satisfied, the old man sat down.

I turned my head when someone stepped through the door behind the assembly. Jack dipped his hand in the holy water font, blessed himself, and slipped into a back pew. I wished he'd heard what old Spiegel had to say.

"Be that as it may, Monsignior," the archbishop retorted, emboldened by the protest. "When secular society leads the way to doing what is right—saying no to homosexual marriage—the church is shamed. We must take a clear stance for truths that are eternal: marriage between a man and a woman, clear pronouncements about the natural order. We have no credibility unless we take action within the priesthood itself. And so the diocese will staunchly enforce the new policy. No homosexual applicants for seminary will be considered. And homosexuality within the priesthood will not be tolerated."

"But Archbishop!" It was Corey. He stood up, two pews in front of me. He was red in the face, from anger, I hoped, and not booze. The day I sent him the nasty e-mail, he'd told me he was back on the wagon. "According to the Vatican, the church is not going to defrock gay priests. There won't be some kind of witch hunt."

"True enough, Father Mulhane. But the Vatican has outlined clear policies against the advocacy of homosexuality in the priesthood and certainly against homosexual behavior."

"I support rights for all people," Corey shot back, clearly taking this new policy as an affront to his affiliation with gay groups.

The archbishop wouldn't budge. "Human rights are one thing, Father Mulhane. Advocacy for homosexuals is another."

"You do want a witch hunt," Corey blurted, furious. "You want to reenact the inquisition." He stumbled past the other priests in the pew and marched out of the chapel.

The archbishop looked a little chastened at being compared to an inquisitor. His tone softened as he continued, "There is a practical reason as well as a spiritual reason for enforcing this policy. Such affairs can only lead to devastating unhappiness, as well as to scandal."

A murmur passed through the group.

The archbishop raised his hand to quiet the priests. "I have a duty to say this. I do it as your shepherd. I do it out of concern for your physical and spiritual safety. If any of you has secrets about sexual misconduct, please, please come to me. And if anyone here knows of someone who has committed this sin, he has an obligation to come forward and tell me the truth."

I was stunned. So was everyone else, evidently. No one muttered a word.

"I realize the risk I'm taking," he continued. "I have no desire to set you against your brothers. But I must appeal to our Lord's words about fraternal correction. If you know of someone guilty of this sin, confront them. Urge them to come to me. If they refuse, you must come to me yourself. It could be a matter of life and death."

Fat Reggie Lutz raised his hand. I expected his usual sanctimonious drivel, but Reggie looked pale and spoke haltingly. "What will happen to the person?" he said. "Will he be given a second chance?"

"No." The archbishop spoke firmly.

Reggie look worried. Did he know someone else's secret? Or did he have his own?

"I realize what I'm asking of you." The archbishop directed his words to Reggie. Then he turned his eyes to the whole group. "But I have a sacred obligation to say this. And you all have a sacred obligation to do what is right. I believe with all my heart that we can survive this horrible scandal in the church. The Holy Spirit will preserve the church. And every time we act in truth and justice, we act in accord with the Holy Spirit."

When the archbishop dismissed the priests, I wanted to get as far away from him as possible. Jack evidently did, too, because by the time I got up and turned around he was already gone. I was starting after him when the archbishop called me. Reluctantly, I held back and let the others pass out of the pew.

"I need to talk to you in my office," the archbishop said with gravity.

So this was it, I thought. He'd found out about Jack and me, and he was giving me walking papers.

We proceeded in silence through the corridor and past the reception desk. I prepared myself for the worst. I wouldn't demean myself by lying. I'd tell the archbishop the truth and let the chips fall where they may.

"Have a seat," the archbishop said, gesturing to an armchair. He sat in the chair facing me. Glancing at the painting of the Assumption of the Virgin, he collected himself before speaking. "Chris, I want you to hear my confession."

I was dumbfounded. This was the last thing in the world I expected to hear. I managed to make a coherent response. "Wouldn't it be better for you to go to someone else? Someone you don't work with?"

The archbhishop shook his head. "I trust you."

I wanted to laugh in his face. But I didn't have the guts. "All right," I said.

I was horrified when the archbishop got up and knelt on the carpet by my chair. I made the sign of the cross over his shiny bald head as he launched into the usual formula.

"Bless me, Father, for I have sinned. It has been two weeks since my last confession." He hesitated. "It's about Edward. About his reason for taking his life."

My self-consciousness evaporated with the words. My body tensed as I listened.

"A month ago, Edward came to me and admitted that he'd had an illicit relationship with another man. I'm not breaking the seal of confession by saying this. Edward didn't tell me this in confession—as you know, I don't hear the confessions of my priests. I can't be put in a position of guarding their secrets if they are violating canon law or civil law. I reminded Edward of that before he shared the information. He insisted on telling me. He said he wanted me to hear the truth from his lips—before I heard from someone else."

"Why was he afraid of that?"

"Because Edward stopped seeing the man. He told him they had made a mistake and warned him to stay away. The man assaulted Edward. And he threatened to go public. That's why I sent you to search the rectory for any incriminating evidence."

I was at a loss for words. I stared at the archbishop's bald head, trying to absorb his confession. "Why don't you sit down, Archbishop?" I finally said. My anger had subsided. Maybe his pronouncement had more to do with his own fear and guilt than with mean-spirited bigotry.

The archbishop got up and returned to his chair. He meekly folded his hands on his lap and sat with feet together on the floor. "I felt sorry for him, Chris. He swore that this relationship was over."

"So how have you sinned?" I was puzzled.

"I should have suspended Edward immediately. To send a clear message. And to avoid the scandal set in motion by the filth written on the parish garage—apparently by Edward's partner in sin, though I'm mystified by why he felt the need to carry out his threat to expose Edward after his death. Maybe someone else is responsible for the scrawl, someone who knew about the illicit relations. I'm sure whoever wrote the graffiti has contributed to the gossip. The president of St. Mary's parish council told me he'd received an anonymous note about Edward's affair, as had several other members of the parish."

So the scandal was all the archbishop cared about—not Eddie's tormented soul. I'd given him the benefit of a doubt, hoping he'd conclude his confession by admitting he'd somehow failed Eddie.

After he made his Act of Contrition, I mumbled an absolution and escaped from the oppressive room.

My head was swimming with information, and I returned to the chapel to think everything through. The overcast sky shed gray light into the room. I sat in a back pew, staring up at the clouds, visible through the clear windows beneath the tentlike ceiling.

So the rumors were true. Just before his death, Eddie had been involved with someone. I could only imagine how guilt-ridden he must have been. Chances were, he'd only slept with the man once or twice before breaking off their affair.

As disturbing as the archbishop's news had been, I realized there was nothing I could or should do. I got up and went to find Jack. I wanted to know his reaction to Koch's pronouncement in the chapel.

Outside his door, I listened. I didn't want to wake him if he was taking a Sunday nap. He'd looked tired at the meeting. But I did hear noise inside the apartment. It sounded like Jack was retching. Finding the door unlocked, I went in and rushed to the bathroom, the source of the sound.

Jack was kneeling in front of the toilet in his T-shirt.

I yanked a damp towel from the towel bar by the sink and handed it to him. "Are you okay?"

He nodded, wiping his face. The sour smell in the room almost made me sick to my stomach. I flushed the toilet.

"Is it the flu?" I said, feeling his forehead. "You don't have a fever."

Jack shrugged. His eyes were watery. He looked blanched.

It struck me that maybe the archbishop's announcement had prompted his sickness. Maybe he finally saw the futility of trying to live a double life in the priesthood. Watching him wipe his face, I felt a perverse tingle of hope. But I told myself I was an idiot for expecting Jack to think like me. He'd probably eaten bad food or contracted some kind of stomach virus.

I finally helped him to his feet. While he cleaned up, I untwisted the blankets shoved to the bottom of his bed and straightened his pillows. When he finished in the bathroom, he climbed into bed, and I pulled the covers up over him.

When I started to leave, he grabbed my hand. "Stay with me," he said, his voice hoarse.

So I lay down next to him, and we both fell asleep.

THAT EVENING, AS we watched TV in my apartment, Jack seemed better. But still he looked defeated. More than anything in the world, I wanted to wrap my arms around him. I wanted to forget my resolution and give myself to him forever. But I told myself that the struggle would get easier. That with time, I could love him without desiring him. That now, as he struggled against whatever secret demon possessed him, I had to be the strong one or we would both be lost.

At ten, Jack returned to his apartment. I got in bed and tossed and turned for hours. When I finally fell asleep, a scene that seemed as much memory as dream played though my unconscious mind. A solid-blue sky loomed above me. Then there was the smell of freshly mown grass, tracked in straight lines across the open fields around St. John's. And the balmy air and the lush spring foliage.

I felt confused, thinking that the last time I'd set foot outdoors, frozen snow lay on the ground and the cold air had made my nose run.

But the scene in front of me was perfectly right. Shirtless boys sprinted on the 880 track. Coach Maher, tan and blond, held a stopwatch at the finish line. At one end of the field in the middle of the track, a three-legged race advanced, and at the other end a wheelbarrow race was in progress. Half-dressed boys clustered and cheered and roughhoused.

It was the St. John's annual May Day festival.

Gripping a rope, I faced the opposing team on the other side of the muddy ditch. They wore gold shorts, and my team wore blue. St. John's colors. The faces of Ben Garris, Tom Hurley, Steve Kalowski, and the others, all squinting in the sun, were clear. Their long hair, plastered on their sweaty foreheads, was tied back or bound by headbands and bandanas. But the sun washed out the face of the first opponent in line. The skinny but sinewy arms and the appendix scar belonged to Jack. And surely it was Jack tugging the rope. His voice cheered on his team and taunted his opponents. It was Jack. But ten yards away, another Jack lay on the grass, basking in the sun. The same sinewy arms absorbed the rays. His sunglasses made him movie-star sexy.

But how could Jack lie there and also face me across the brown ditch? How could he taunt me like this, no longer in fun, but with cruelty?

"You're a fucking queer, Seib. I'm sending you to hell."

Jack's team roared. They yanked the rope. I had been leaning back, my bare heels digging into the mud, but the tug sent me flying forward. My teammates followed, piling on me in the ditch.

The opponents jumped in after them. The boys lobbed mud at one another. They shoved each other down. Jack—it was Jack, wasn't it?—straddled me in the mud, locked my arms back, and suddenly, painfully entered me.

"Jesus, Jack!" I yelled, looking to the other Jack for help. But the sun god had disappeared.

When I opened my eyes, I found Jack in bed next to me. He'd apparently returned to my apartment during the night—just wanting to be next to me. He slept peacefully on top of the teal comforter, his head resting on his arm. He looked so sweet. I wanted to kiss him. But I didn't let myself. I got up, covered him with a blanket, and climbed back into bed, immediately falling back to sleep.

AFTER OVER A week of good behavior, Jack asked me to go out—as friends. He'd shown admirable restraint, and I guess I had, too. Of course, I wanted nothing more than to go out with him, even though my better judgment warned me it was too soon to try anything that could easily turn romantic. But I rationalized away my doubts, and we made plans to go to a winter film festival at a drive-in theater.

On Friday evening, I was in the staff kitchen dumping steaming microwave popcorn into a Tupperware container. I filled a cooler with ice from the ice-maker in the big industrial kitchen next door and filled the cooler with beer. Jack helped me carry the refreshments and blankets to the pickup, parked in front of St. John's.

"I told you the snow would stop," Jack said as he climbed in. He wore his leather jacket and ski cap. He started the engine and turned up the heat.

"This is still crazy," I said when we were on the road, hugging myself to warm up. "It's freezing out. I can't believe they keep the drive-in open in this weather."

"I hear it's a popular place. The kids like to make out under the blankets."

I figured this information came from Danny, but I didn't bring up his name.

We reached the Lawrence drive-in in twenty minutes. Cars packed the huge, snow-covered area in front of the screen. The two features were old Dracula films, the first with Gary Oldman as the Count and the second with William Marshall in his first *Blacula* movie. Most of the cars were filled with kids—both coupled and in rowdy packs.

"Are we the only ones here over twenty-five?" I said with dismay.

"Relax," Jack said, reaching back in the cooler for a beer. He handed one to me. "It'll be fun."

We switched on the portable heater we'd picked up at the concession stand and spread a blanket over our laps. All through the first movie, car doors opened and shut as kids trailed to the refreshment counter and bathrooms. The kids in a battered van next to us passed around joints and screamed obscenities at the screen. In the car ahead of us, a boy and girl slid down the backseat and sent the car rocking.

Jack seemed more content than I'd seen him since our official breakup, clearly happy to be with me. I longed to hold his hand under the blanket. During a gory murder on the screen, I involuntarily grabbed his arm. He turned and searched my eyes, as though asking permission to hold me. I released him quickly.

By the time Dracula wept over his dead paramour at the end of the first movie, I was feeling the effects of the beer. Jack must have been, too. Suddenly he snuggled against me, and kissed me on the lips. I thought I'd melt into his arms.

Suddenly a car horn blared behind us. I drew away from Jack. But it was too late. Two big guys in ball caps appeared on either side of the pickup. The one on Jack's side wore a camouflage jacket. They pounded the windshield with their gloved fists.

"Hey, fags. Get the hell out of here." They started to rock the pickup. The stoned kids in the next car cheered them on.

My heart was racing. "Let's go," I blurted, scared to death.

Jack reached in the glove compartment.

"What's that?" I said, straining to make out the object. "Is that a gun? Jesus, Jack! Are you insane?" I grabbed Jack's arm, desperate to stop him. "Come on. Let's just leave."

Jack jerked his arm away. He opened his door and climbed out.

When the boys saw the gun in his hand, they backed away from the car.

The brawny kid on the driver's side raised his hands to calm Jack. "Hey, man. We're cool. Get a grip. See, we're leaving."

"Stop it! Leave them alone," a girl called from the car behind them. She and another girl had jumped out and stood behind the opened doors.

Jack aimed the gun at the boy in the camouflage jacket. "If you fuckers wanna play, we can play," he said, stepping toward him.

I couldn't believe what I was seeing. I had to stop this—somehow. I got out of the car. "Come on, Jack," I said, my breath smoking in the cold. Nervous perspiration dripped down my sides. "Put it down. They're leaving."

Jack looked like he had snapped. He clenched his teeth. His eyes were wild.

"Shoot him, lone ranger," a boy in the next car shouted. The other kids echoed the command.

"Please, Jack!" I pleaded.

Jack seemed oblivious to me. "Tell me you're fags, too," he commanded the kids.

"What?" The broad-faced kid on my side of the car stepped forward menacingly.

Jack turned the gun on him. "I said to tell me that you're a couple of fags. Now."

The kid stopped in his tracks.

"Just say it," I said. "Please." I'd never begged so desperately in my whole life.

The boys glanced at each other and mumbled the words.

"Louder," Jack said

"We're fags!" they shouted.

The stoned kids giggled and yelled obscenities.

I noticed that the girlfriends had disappeared, undoubtedly to get help. "Let's go, Jack. Fast."

"Get the hell out of here." Jack brandished his gun at the kids. They cautiously walked away, looking over their shoulders.

We got into the truck. Jack tossed out the portable heater and tore off through the snow covered gravel and out the exit.

My heart thudded. Out of danger now, anger rushed through me. "What in the hell are you doing? You could have killed somebody."

Without answering me, Jack opened the glove compartment and placed the gun inside.

"Jack! What is going on?"

Jack cast me a frighteningly smug glance—the glance of a criminal proud of his crime.

"Do you even have a license for the gun?" I sighed, glancing in the side-view mirror to see if we were being followed. I was relieved to find that the closest headlights were in the distance. "You know, your great goal of sainthood—a little humility might be the way to achieve it."

"Humility's not the same as humiliation."

"So it's humiliating when a punk calls you a fag, but not when the fucking church calls you a pervert condemned to hell."

Jack leveled a hateful gaze at me. "It's your church, too. I don't see you making waves."

The words twisted like a cold blade in my belly. "This is all wrong," I blurted, staring at the road. "Us. It can't work."

"Don't say that," Jack shouted, pounding the dashboard. "Don't say that."

"Or what? Are you gonna pull your gun on me?" Rage had overcome my fear of Jack. Rage at the punks. Rage at Jack for scaring me.

As we rode home in silence, I could see Jack's agitation. He rubbed his face. He smoked. At one point he seemed to be crying. But I wouldn't let myself give in. He'd scared me too much.

When we pulled into the parking garage, I turned to him and, without a drop of mercy, said, "Stay away from me."

Leaving him there to collect our stuff, I took the elevator up to our floor, shut myself in my apartment, and sobbed like a baby.

Jack Canston's Journal

January 26

They were the ones! There in the dark—they were the same punks. But this time I was in charge, not them. I had the gun. The one thing my old man ever gave me that has made a fucking difference in my life. I would have blown them away if Chris hadn't been there. I didn't care what happened to me for it. I didn't think about it. It wouldn't have been premeditated, so my culpability would have been mitigated—isn't that what my old theology profs used to say?

But Chris was there. He saved them. He saved me from killing the wrong punks, even if they seemed the same. Then he cut me off. He's probably right. How can I blame him? But how can I be near him and not touch him? I'll be even crazier. I'll turn the gun on myself.

10

THE NEXT MORNING, I stared out at the cold, gray day. Everything seemed lifeless—the dingy white fields, the bare trees, the sunless sky.

I couldn't get the sight of Jack and the gun out of my mind. I kept telling myself that he wouldn't have used it. That he had just wanted to scare them. Of course, he'd hated them in the moment. Maybe they were symbols of the Vatican, calling him a faggot. No, that's what I felt, not Jack. At least I felt it afterward, once Jack's craziness didn't claim all my attention.

Had I really told him to stay away? Had I really meant it? God, no. But what else could I say? If I got caught up in his pain, I got stuck forever in the life he could never leave. Sacrificing for him meant sacrificing all self-respect. I'd live up to the Vatican's label—intrinsically disordered.

A GROUP OF seniors from St. Joseph High School was due to arrive that day for an overnight retreat. I was scheduled to give talks and offer spiritual direction. The distraction would be good for me. Jack would be busy at Santa Rosa's all weekend. The time apart would help me put everything in perspective. Everything would work out. Somehow.

I greeted the group of thirty kids, accompanied by two-tough looking nuns in veils and short, modernized habits. I led them to their rooms, the boys in one dormitory building, the girls in the other. I gave them housekeeping instructions and took them on a tour of St. John's before letting them get ready for the opening mass.

An hour later, they'd assembled in the chapel. Two boys and a girl led the singing with guitars. As I looked out over the group, I found it hard to believe that when they were born I was already on the verge of ordination. They seemed older, their postures and expressions somehow betraying their sexual experience. A few of the bulky boys with buzzed heads looked like college football players. A couple of others, disheveled and long-haired, had a studied sensuality. The girls, in jeans and sweaters, might have belonged to a college sorority.

The group was supposed to spend the afternoon in silent reflection after my first talk on spirituality, but when I went out to walk in the fields where I could think about Jack, I spotted a few kids smoking on the handball court. They hid their cigarettes behind their backs and nervously waved to me. I nodded to show I was cool about it and kept trudging along.

I wanted to call Jack. Twice I hit the automatic dial button programmed with his number. Then I hung up before his phone could ring. What did I plan to say? I didn't mean it? I love you?

After dinner, I spoke to the kids about faith. "It's not a bunch of doctrines that you believe," I explained. "It's not like a possession you clutch and guard like money. Faith means loving when you don't feel like it. It's not letting fear decide what you do. It's moving towards others, towards everything that is life-giving." Of course I was thinking of Jack. But was moving toward him life-giving or a recipe for destruction?

One of the football players raised his hand. "You mean it's not a sin if you don't believe all the stuff the church teaches?"

"No."

One of the nuns suddenly bolted to her feet. A shock of gray hair escaped her veil. Her square jaw and crooked nose made her look like a boxer. "Father doesn't mean you should dismiss church teaching," she said, frowning at me. "He means we all have to ask questions in order to clarify what the church teaches. Isn't that true, Father?"

I considered backing off, but I didn't. "Faith isn't a bunch of dogmas. That's what I'm saying."

The nun glared at me. "I'm sorry, that's not what we teach at St. Joseph's. Keep that in mind, boys and girls."

After the presentation, I heard confessions for an hour. The sins were predictable—getting drunk, lying to parents, missing Sunday mass, having sex. The kids took advantage of the anonymity to clear their adolescent consciences. When I emerged from the confessional, I was ready for a drink.

But as I started out of the dark chapel, I heard someone crying. The flickering sanctuary candle revealed the silhouette of a girl kneeling near the tabernacle, and I went to her.

"What's the matter?" I said, touching her shoulder.

She shook her head in despair. "I'm an abomination. I'm going to hell."

As soon as she said it, I knew, but I had to let her tell me. Full of tenderness, I sat next to her in the dark. "What's your name?" I said, gently.

"Lauren," she whispered. She had a pretty, freckled face and wore a sweatshirt with a bulldog on the front, the mascot of St. Joe's High. Her eyes were large and round, a child's innocent eyes.

"Why are you an abomination?"

Lauren lowered her gaze in shame.

"It's all right," I said, touching her cool hand.

"I'm in love with another girl. But she broke up with me." She barely choked the words out, as tears came.

Squeezing her hand, I let her sob.

Finally she calmed down and wiped her nose with the sleeve of her sweatshirt. "Carly said we'd go to hell if we kept it up. But I feel like I'm in hell now. Is she right, Father? Am I going to hell?"

"Of course not." My heart was breaking for her.

"Doesn't the Church say I am?"

"No. The Church just says you have to be celibate."

"So Carly and I could never be together."

"Not according to the Church." I had to tell her the truth. It wouldn't do any good to sugarcoat the Church's teaching. I wanted her to protest the injustice of it, so I could agree with her.

"You said we don't have to believe everything the Church teaches."

"That's right." I fought an impulse to tell the truth about myself, something I'd never done to a layperson, let alone a teenager in need. But looking at the pain in her face, I finally couldn't stop myself. "I'm gay, Lauren."

The admission surprised her. She stared at me, with those big round eyes. Then she glanced away.

"What's wrong?"

"Some of the boys were making fun of you. They thought you were gay. I didn't stand up for you."

People can tell, I thought, panicking. And apparently my Roman collar didn't protect me from wagging tongues. Although my fears had flared from time to time, this was the first time they were ever confirmed.

"But you're celibate," Lauren said, despairingly. "So the church's teaching doesn't affect you."

I wondered at her innocence. I felt like the biggest hypocrite on the face of the earth, but this wasn't the time to bare my soul and disabuse her of her naïveté. I was silent for a long moment before rallying myself to do my job. "You'll find someone to love, Lauren," I finally said. "Maybe it'll be Carly, maybe it'll be someone else. When you do, go for it. God will be with you both."

THE NEXT AFTERNOON, the retreat over and the last kid on the bus heading home, I crawled into bed, exhausted. When I woke up, the room was black. The glowing numbers on the digital alarm clock said it was seven o'clock. I'd only slept for two hours. Jack should be back by now. I had to go to him. I couldn't stop myself.

The dark corridor stirred a familiar sense of loneliness. On Sunday nights during high school years, when my dad dropped me off at St. John's after a weekend at home, I was often one of the first boys back. The halls were empty. The chapel was empty. The linoleum floors of the dormitory, waxed over the weekend, shone like cold marble under the harsh fluorescent lights. I always felt vaguely abandoned in the very place that, during the light and noise of daytime, felt like the best home in the world. It was the shadow side of St. John's, which spoke to the frightened, shadow side of my own soul.

I knocked on Jack's door and called his name. There was no response. The door was unlocked. I entered the living room and switched on a lamp. The few books that Jack kept on the shelves were gone. The desk, usually piled with clothes and papers, was clear. In the bedroom, the mattress had been stripped. Jack's rosary and alarm clock were no longer on the nightstand. Most of the clothes were gone from the closet, and the top drawer of the dresser, where Jack kept his underwear and socks, was empty.

Panicking, I went to the phone on the living room desk and called Jack's cell phone. After several rings, the recorded message played. And I left my own message, trying to sound calm. "Jack, where are you? What's going on? Call me."

Back in my apartment, I stayed near the phone. I paced in front of the gurgling aquarium, stopping every few minutes to stare out the window at the drive, hoping to see Jack's pickup. After half an hour, I couldn't take it anymore. I put on my coat and rushed down to the garage.

Doing eighty on the interstate, I arrived in Topeka in forty-five minutes, but the trip seemed to take longer than usual. At Santa Rosa's I pulled up next to Jack's pickup, parked in the rectory driveway. The building had been framed and roofed, and masons had started the brickwork, but there were no windows or doors.

The windows of the church were dark and the front doors locked. When I went around to the side of the church, I saw a light in the basement window and knocked on it through the security bars. "Jack! Are you there?"

I glanced around at the empty parking lot. A woman in the house next door climbed down the back steps with a bag of garbage and lugged it to the alley. I waited until she'd gone back into the house before knocking on the window again.

Finally, it slid open. Jack's face appeared. "Please, go home, Chris."

"What are you doing? Let me in."

He yielded. "Go to the back door."

Jack let me in, locking the door behind us, and led me into a large hall glowing under fluorescent lights. Folding tables and chairs were stacked on one side of the room under a colorful image of Our Lady of Guadalupe painted on the cinderblock wall. In a corner of the other side of the room, a twin mattress lay on the linoleum tiles. An upside-down plastic crate next to it held the things usually on Jack's bed table. Jack's clothes lay in piles on the floor.

"What are you doing?" I said, waving my hand toward Jack's things.

Jack stood in his stocking feet with his arms dangling at his sides, looking helpless in the middle of the large room. He wore faded blue jeans and his gray sweatshirt, and the stubble was heavy on his face at the late hour.

"I can't be around you if I can't have you." He shook his head. "I'm messed up. It's better for me to be away from you. I can hang out here until the rectory's finished."

"This is crazy. You can't stay here like this."

Jack rubbed his face. He found his cigarettes in the pocket of his coat, which lay on the bed, and lit one. He opened a folding chair, turned it backward, and straddled it, resting his arms on the back.

I unzipped my coat and opened a chair for myself, sitting down. I knew I had to push now or we'd keep spinning in place forever. "I want you to tell me something. I want you to tell me why you were in the state hospital."

Jack looked startled.

"I saw an envelope with the hospital's return address on it. In Koch's office. I saw it the night you found me in there."

"You were searching my records?" Jack said in a strangely fearful way.

"I needed to find out what you're running from. But there was nothing in the envelope."

"That's because I took it." Jack dropped his cigarette on the floor and stepped on it. "In case anybody started looking." He got up. He seemed desperate now, as though there was no escaping from the truth.

"Why were you in the hospital?"

He squeezed his eyes shut and rubbed his temples.

I softened. "Tell me, Jack."

He looked at me now, hesitating. Then he sat down, looking resigned and determined to answer, which he finally did in a deliberate monotone, staring into the air. "Last year, my brother Ben and I went hunting in Wyoming. Near Jackson Hole. We had Ben's dog with us. A big yellow lab named Sam. Ben loved that dog. We didn't realize how close we were to the road. Sam just took off after a jackrabbit. We heard brakes screech. Then a crash. When we got to him, he was out in the middle of the road. The car had thrown him and taken off. Ben ran out to him right in the path of an oncoming truck. It hit him. Ten feet in front of me."

"Jesus, Jack."

"He was dead before the ambulance got there." Choked up, Jack paused. "I lost it," he said softly. "I had a breakdown. I checked into the pysch unit at the hospital. I was there for six weeks."

I stared at him, full of compassion.

"I guess it helped. Got some antidepressants. Got some therapy. Started smoking. Real smart, huh?" He forced a chuckle.

"That's why you lost it the night we saw the dog in the road." Now it all made sense—his bizarre behavior, his shattered nerves. No wonder he had succumbed to Danny. In my heart, I forgave him once and for all.

"You must have thought I was a lunatic."

"Why didn't you just tell me?"

"I can't explain it. I tried. I finally figured, what's the difference? It wouldn't fix the problem. You'd be stuck with it, too."

"I wanna be stuck with it. What I don't want is to be shut out."

"Shutting out is what I do," Jack confessed.

"It doesn't have to be. The priesthood taught you that. It taught all of us that. Put up walls. Don't let anyone see that you're human."

Jack's eyes suddenly gleamed with a kind of devilish determination. "Let's leave it," he said.

"Leave what?" I asked, confused. Then the strange gleam made me realize what he was saying. "You mean leave the priesthood?" I couldn't believe I was hearing this. It was all I'd wanted to hear for months, and now he was saying it! The most amazing hope soared in me, hope against every ounce of sense that urged me to put on the brakes, to think through everything carefully, assess objectively Jack's own desperation. "Do you really mean it?"

He got up, took me by the hand, and pulled me to my feet, gazing unabashedly into my eyes. "Yes," he said, kissing my lips and leading me to the mattress. He turned off the lights and stripped off his clothes and then mine.

And I let him. I would have let him do whatever he desired in that moment—I wanted him so much and was so outrageously sure that everything could be all right now. He'd explained it all. The horrible death of his brother. The shock. The guilt. My God, wasn't it enough to drive the most stable person over the edge?

Very tenderly, we consummated our new bond on the bare mattress. We were married and on our way to a brave new world.

Afterward, I lay stroking Jack's furry chest, trying to fathom the nightmare he'd experienced. I felt like the lover of a broken soldier who'd witnessed the horrors of war. A scene from *Othello* popped into my mind, all those years after reading the play in college: Othello's angry father-in-law had just accused the black Moor of seducing his daughter, Desdemona. Othello defended himself by explaining that he hadn't forced her to marry him, that his tragic war stories had won her heart. I looked up the scene later. In that sweet moment in the basement of the church, Jack could have used Othello's words about Desdemona to describe my feelings for him:

My story being done,
She gave me for my pains a world of kisses.
She swore in faith 'twas strange, 'twas passing strange;
'Twas pitiful, 'twas wondrous pitiful.
She wished she had not heard it; yet she wished
That heaven had made her such a man.

11

"TAKE ANOTHER ONE, Father," Debbie said, flushed as always. She offered me a plastic container full of brownies. Alberta and I sat on the lime-green couch in her office, talking to Fran Becker, the editor of the diocesan paper. "You can have it for an afternoon snack."

"Well, if you insist." I smiled.

I was still high on the happiness of the promise Jack had made the night before. The weather reflected my mood. Following days of cloudy skies, sunlight poured into Alberta's office, which also seemed amazingly cheery. A new schefflera with thick, glossy foliage drank in the rays. A new poster hung on the wall next to the one with the flower. In a child's bold printing, the words "When Life Gives You Lemons, Make Lemonade" formed an arch over a lemon tree. I couldn't have said it better.

After Alberta and Fran declined a second brownie, Debbie waved and went back to her office.

"I just don't know what to do," Fran said, swallowing the last bite of her brownie. She sat in the chair across from the sofa, a folded newspaper on her lap. She was a serious-looking woman in her forties with high cheekbones and large, expressive eyes. She wore a turquoise necklace and earrings made by a local Native American tribe. "The *Mustard Seed* has to address this article in the *Star.* The archdiocese has a responsibility to make sense of this for people. "

"Let me see it," Alberta said, reaching for the Kansas City newspaper. She wore a white turtleneck and a black wool skirt. "My God! This is a travesty." She shook her head.

"I know. I just can't believe it," Fran said. "The Vatican has ordered every diocese to inspect its seminaries. What exactly is the archbishop supposed to be looking for? Seminarians that like show tunes or watch *Will and Grace* reruns?"

I laughed. What the hell did I care anymore if the church was launching an inquisition to purge seminaries of intrinsically disordered candidates for the priesthood?

Alberta frowned with disapproval at my nonchalance. "All this will do is drive gay seminarians deeper into the closet. They have to be celibate anyway. What difference does it make if they're gay or not? This new mandate will confuse people. They'll think being gay is the same thing as being a sexual predator. The Vatican is just looking for a scapegoat to save it from the national scandal."

"Exactly," Fran said, brushing crumbs from her lap. "The archbishop needs to explain all that that in a formal letter in the *Mustard Seed.*"

"Like that will happen!" I snorted. "He's ordered every pastor to read the new mandate from the pulpit. I doubt that the shepherd's worried about protecting his black sheep."

"He must feel some compassion for his gay priests," Fran said. Then she added doubtfully, "At least he should."

"The road to hell is paved with good intentions," I said.

Fran nodded sadly. "Well," she said, rising and brushing crumbs from her slacks. "It's a shame. I've gotta get back to work. Deadline, you know."

When Fran had returned to her office, I got up and closed the door. I must have been beaming when I turned to Alberta and smiled.

She folded her arms and studied me with a sideways glance. "Okay, what is it?"

"I'm gonna do it," I said.

Alberta wrinkled her forehead in confusion.

"Get off the pot," I explained. "I'm gonna get off the pot."

I dropped into the armchair and told her everything about the dramatic weekend, ending with Jack's declaration.

"Whoa!" Alberta said, raising her hand. "He pulled a gun on two kids? He *is* crazy."

I hurried to Jack's defense. "He just fell apart. After what happened with his brother, his world crumbled. He's still recovering."

"He could have killed them. Then what? You would have been implicated, too."

"He wouldn't have done that. He just wanted to scare them. And who knows what they might have done to us?"

Alberta shook her head. "I don't buy it. He could have started the car and taken off. He could have picked up his cell phone and called the police—or just laid on the horn to attract attention. Anything but pull out a gun. Sweet Jesus!"

"You weren't there," I blurted, angry at her for trying to ruin my dream. "These two punks were ready to do some fag bashing."

"Stop and listen to yourself, Chris. Why are you defending this insanity?"

I felt chastened. Of course she was right. My initial response had been exactly like hers. I yielded the point and took a different tactic. "He's so torn up inside, Alberta. He's striking out."

Alberta touched my hand. "Then he needs to get help," she reasoned. "From someone neutral."

How could I object?

"And being involved with you only creates more stress. For him and you."

"That's why we have to leave the priesthood."

She leveled her hazel eyes at me. "Do you really think he'll leave? After everything he's told you?"

"He promised." I suddenly felt like a little boy trying to convince himself that his daddy really would take him to the moon.

"Maybe you're ready to leave. *Maybe.* But I'm willing to bet that he has no intention of leaving."

I sat there quietly, hating her for saying this.

"You wanna tell me to go to hell, don't you?" she finally asked.

"Yes," I said. And I meant it.

I SPENT THE afternoon gloomily taking inventory of guest supplies and following the maintenance man through the buildings to prioritize repairs. The nuts and bolts of administration usually exasperated me, but today they were a good distraction. I didn't want to think about Alberta's observations. I didn't want to scrutinize Jack's intentions or my own motives. I clung to my dream of Jack and me making a life for ourselves, no longer hiding, no longer under the steel fist of the church.

I made meatloaf for dinner and shared it with the archbishop in the small staff dining room. The archbishop opened a bottle of Chianti that he'd brought back from a recent trip to Rome. I tried not to hate him for starting his inquisition. I tried to remind myself that this kind man had acted from fear and ignorance, but I couldn't shake my resentment. We ate quietly, chatting about neutral topics. Somehow I got through dinner. Then, taking the archbishop up on his offer to do the dishes, I left him in the kitchen, went to my apartment, and watched TV.

Jack was teaching a confirmation class at Santa Rosa's and wasn't due home until late. I didn't bother watching for his truck, so when ten o'clock rolled around with no sign of him, I wondered if he'd returned and gone to his apartment. As I headed down the corridor, I heard shouting from his rooms. I listened outside his door.

"Godamn you! You're supposed to be on my side." The voice belonged to Danny Flores. "You're supposed to—"

"Calm down, Danny," Jack said.

Jack mumbled something that I couldn't understand. I pressed my ear to the door but caught only a phrase here and there. *Be smart. God's will. Making sacrifices.*

Danny broke down. His sobs were muffled. Jack was probably embracing him. I raised my hand to pound on the door, but I caught myself. Jack had come back, hadn't he? He had promised to start a new life with me. Intruding would mean I didn't trust him. How could we build a life on suspicion?

I went back to my apartment and forced myself to wait for Jack to appear, which he finally did, an hour later.

He plopped down on the sofa, where I was stretched out, reading a magazine. He kicked off his shoes and propped his legs on the coffee table. I rested my feet on his lap.

He still wore his clerical shirt, opened at the neck, the white tab removed from the collar and sticking out of his breast pocket. He lit a cigarette and rested his head on the back of the couch.

"You look exhausted," I said. "Hard day at the parish?"

"Long day." Jack threw back his head and exhaled a stream of smoke. "Lots of people with problems. One married couple at each other's throat. How about you?"

"Just boring maintenance stuff." I thought about Alberta's words and examined him for some confirmation that he intended to keep his promise about leaving the priesthood—and for some explanation about Danny's visit. I could see he was clearly content to be back with me. And he showed no signs of agitation. But why didn't he broach the subject that should be on both of our minds? After sitting quietly for a few moments, I tested him. "Just think, maybe next year at this time, we'll be in our own house."

Jack closed his eyes without responding.

"It scares me," I said. "I don't have a clue how I'll make a living. I guess it's something we should both start planning. Do you think we'd be ready to leave in six months?"

He remained silent.

I finally pressed him. "What's wrong, Jack? You haven't changed your mind, have you?"

"I'm tired. That's all," he said without opening his eyes. "I can't think about it now."

I stewed for a minute, deciding that Danny was to blame for claiming Jack's interest and energy. "I went to your apartment a little while ago. I heard Danny's voice. He seemed upset."

Jack mumbled an "Uh huh" without any move to elaborate.

"Where is he? Is he staying in one of the dorms?"

"He came in his sister's car. He went home."

"But why was he here? You're not still counseling him, are you?"

He looked away, guiltily.

"I can't believe it!"

"He's got problems, okay?" Jack snapped. "He needs my help."

Shaking my head in disbelief, I got up and moved to an armchair.

"What's wrong?" Jack said.

"Come on, Jack. Do I have to explain?"

Jack leaned forward, gazing at me earnestly. "You don't have to worry. I promise. I'll never cross the line again."

"Just leave," I said, exasperated.

Jack ground his cigarette in an ashtray, picked up his shoes, and left the apartment without another word.

I let him go. We were both tired and irritable. In the morning, everything would be better.

When I went to bed, I thrashed for a long time before finally falling into a fitful sleep. Then I had a horrible dream. I was chasing Jack through the woods, yelling for him to stop before he got to the highway. But it was too late. He lunged out to the road. Brakes squealed. A sickening thud followed. I found his bloody, twisted body splayed on the pavement.

IN THE MORNING, I woke up feeling anxious. To calm myself, I swam laps for an hour. When I got to my office, the message indicator on my phone was flashing. I picked up the receiver and hit the play button.

"Father Seib, this is Danny Flores." Danny sounded like he'd been crying. "I really need to talk to you. It's very important. Please call me as soon as you get this message. Oh, and whatever you do, don't tell Father Jack I called."

I jotted down the number that Danny left and sat back in my chair. What in the hell was going on? Why keep the message from Jack? I looked up at the laughing Jesus, who seemed to be mocking me now: *So, you thought your dreams could come true? You thought your first and only love had returned to carry you away? Dream on!*

I had to talk to Jack. I punched his programmed number on my phone, but the line was busy. I hesitated, then called Danny's number. Danny answered immediately.

"I need to see you, Father."

"That's not a good idea," I said sternly. "What do you want?"

"It's about Father Jack. I'll explain. Just let me talk to you."

"All right," I said, resigned to knowing the worst.

"Can you come here? To my house. I don't have a car."

FOR THE SECOND time that week, I found myself at the Flores house. Despite the cold, Danny greeted me at the door in a tank top that showed off his pectoral muscles and arms—his tattoo prominent. He ushered me into the cramped living room. The floor and chairs were covered with white cartons of new dishes, depicted on the manufacturer's label.

"They're for the restaurant," Danny explained, nodding toward the boxes. "Let's talk in my room."

"No," I said adamantly. "We can talk in the kitchen."

Ignoring my instructions with a smirk, he turned and led the way to the room I had blessed at the request of his mother. Stupid or not, I followed him.

In my last visit there there, I'd been too upset about Jack to notice anything but the bed. Now I saw that the walls were covered with photographs and posters. There were glossy signed photographs of mostly male movie stars, including Brad Pitt, Antonio Banderas, Ben Affleck, and a dozen others. There were posters of the pope—waving from his popemobile, kneeling at the Grotto of Lourdes, laying his hand on the head of a little boy. On one wall, the Virgin of Guadalupe was painted in primary tempera colors. Surrounding the image were handwritten poems and prayers to the Virgin.

But the strangest feature of the room was a boarded window, plastered with apocalyptic bumper stickers: "God's Returning and Is He Mad!"; "The Fires of Hell Are No Joke!"; "God vs. Satan: No Contest"; and the like.

I wanted to bolt from the scary room, but when Danny gestured to an armchair draped with an orange afghan, I sat as directed. Danny sat facing me on the edge of the bed. Our knees almost touched.

"Thanks for coming, Father." His eyes were full of mischief.

"What do you want to tell me, Danny?" I said impatiently.

He took his time answering, looking me over smugly. "What my mom told you about Father Jack and me—it's true. But you should know, he put the moves on me. He's a fucking priest, for God's sake."

"I don't believe you." I started to get up.

He grabbed my arm. "I'm telling you," he blurted angrily, "he sat next to me on the couch and put his hand on my crotch. I was confessing my sins."

I sat back down and scrutinized his face.

"You think I'm lying? Why would I?"

He looked so serious, that for a moment I thought he might be telling the truth. "Why did you come here to the house for confession?" I said.

Danny shrugged. "I wanted to show him my place." When he saw that I was unconvinced, he sized me up. "Look, Father. You can believe me or not, I don't care. It's the truth, and I'm doing my duty to tell someone. I can sleep with a good conscience. So now you deal with it." He folded his arms and glared at me.

I loathed him in that moment—sulking like a spoiled child, indifferent to the harm his words caused as long as he could say them. "Okay," I said, standing up. "I'll deal with it." I turned away from him and walked out the door, half expecting him to yell something hateful after me. But he didn't say a word. He didn't get up to follow me out of the house. But as I walked out the front door and down the porch steps to the car, I knew he was gloating, sitting back and imagining the hell Jack would pay for wounding him.

As I drove home, my whole body felt numb. I was in a trance, unaware of the sleet pelting the windshield, unaware that I was speeding. I didn't register the flashing light in my rearview mirror until the siren wailed. I pulled over to the shoulder and let a stocky cop in sunglasses chew me out and write a ticket.

The incident snapped me back to attention. I started to think logically. What was I afraid of? Danny was a troubled kid. Jack had rebuffed him, and he was striking out. And all the fanfare about the new Vatican mandate had supplied him with perfect ammunition. Danny knew the mere accusation of impropriety could cost Jack dearly.

WHEN JACK GOT home that evening, I apologized for acting like an ass the night before. He kissed me and told me to forget it. He suggested we go get something to eat. We drove to a Vietnamese restaurant in Lawrence.

Sitting in a booth, I told him about Danny's accusation, doing my best to convey my disbelief. I didn't want him to think my suspicion was still alive and well. "I'll bet this is as far as it goes," I said, swallowing a bite of spring roll. "If he'd really wanted to make trouble for you, he would have gone to the archbishop. He just wants to scare you."

In a red sweatshirt, Jack stared at a big smiling Buddha sitting on the floor near the bar. He hadn't touched the dumplings on the little plastic plate with oriental scrolling.

"Maybe you should tell the archbishop," I said. "Before Danny does."

Jack looked at me now, somberly. "He'll suspend me. Automatically. He'd be obligated to report this to the diocesan review board. You think that, with everything going on, they're gonna cut me any slack?"

I knew he was right. "They'll send you back to Montana."

"And Montana will expel me from the priesthood."

"For one mistake?"

"I can't have another mark on my record."

I stared at him, confused. "How can they hold a breakdown against you? Your brother was killed, for God's sake."

Jack averted his eyes.

"What?"

"I tried to commit suicide."

I thought I'd misunderstood. But he looked me in the eye and repeated the words.

"I can't believe you didn't tell me this."

"I wanted to forget it," Jack said gloomily.

"How did you do it?" I said, angry. "I want to know."

Jack studied me, as if to determine whether I was serious.

"I mean it. I want to know."

"Sleeping pills. All right? They pumped my stomach. If I'd had my gun at the time, I'd be dead now."

For the rest of the evening, as we walked through the cold fields and shared drinks in my apartment, I tried to fight off a sense of impending doom. I wondered if Jack was broken beyond repair, if I should throw away my hopes for our future. I kept telling myself that he could get better, now that he had someone to love him. Together, we could work through his emotional turmoil.

We went to bed early and fell immediately asleep. In the middle of the night, the phone rang in the living room. I let the voice mail pick up. Then I got up to listen to the message. There was nothing.

"Who was it?" Jack mumbled when I crawled back into bed.

"No one."

Jack snuggled up to me, his chest against my back, his arm wrapped around me. I lay in his embrace for what felt like hours before my mind quit racing and I finally went back to sleep.

Jack Canston's Journal

January 30

Our Lady of Lourdes answered my prayers. I'll get control back. The nightmares will disappear. I can't thank her for him. He's not in her department, the department of the flesh. But if he wasn't, I'd be tempted to say the Virgin brought us together. Without him, I wouldn't have a snowball's chance in hell to get through this. But he's on the human side of things, not the spiritual. If I'm cured, it will be due to divine power.

12

FOR THE NEXT few days, I was busy enough to keep my mind off everything. I had a hundred things to do in the office, including interviewing applicants for the maintenance position I'd advertised after our old maintenance man resigned.

After meeting three unimpressive candidates, I finally interviewed someone I liked. Mike Finney was a gentle-looking man in his late forties. Despite the cold, he wore a short-sleeved shirt, frayed at the collar but freshly ironed. His grizzled hair and moustache were not closely trimmed. His sleepy-eyed expression and general demeanor suggested a lack of self-consciousness. Very relaxed, he sat back on the couch in my office, his legs crossed.

"The principal of Shonefield Middle School gave you a great recommendation," I said, handing him a mug of coffee and sitting in an armchair. "According to him, you kept the place running like a well-oiled machine. That's a quote."

Mike smiled, exposing a gap between his front teeth. "Sounds like him."

"You were at Shonefield for two years. Where did you work before that?" Finney hadn't turned in his job application yet.

"I guess you really don't recognize me after all these years." There was a faint muddiness in Finney's speech, as though his tongue was swollen. "I graduated from St. John's the year before you came. I was one of the student counselors when you came to the seminary summer camp. I guess you were in eighth grade then. I remember you played the clarinet in the talent show. Squeaked a lot." Mike's blue eyes twinkled playfully.

I laughed, remembering my performance in front of thirty boys. "No, I can't say I do remember you. So, you went on to ordination?"

Mike nodded and sipped his coffee. "In the Wichita diocese. Left the priesthood two years ago and started working at Shonefield."

"As a maintenance man." My surprise must have been obvious.

Mike chuckled. "Big fall from grace, huh?"

I was embarrassed that he'd caught my snobbery.

"Amazing, isn't it?" he laughed. "We learned that ordination makes you a servant of God, but it's a pretty prestigious role, isn't it? Compared to a guy who fixes furnaces."

I nodded. "Sounds like you're happy."

"Yeah. Believe it or not. Getting a job ain't so easy when your only experience is hearing confessions."

"I guess you could have gone into some kind of social work. Counseling, maybe." I always assumed I'd take this route myself if I ever left the priesthood. Lately, I'd been thinking about it a lot. Jack and I needed to make plans.

"You mean go back to school at the age of forty-five?" Mike smiled and shook his head. "I would have been paying off student loans for the rest of my life. Just so I could do what I used to do as a priest. No thanks. I'll take fixing furnaces any day. Thank God, my dad taught me some practical skills."

I suddenly got a sinking feeling in my stomach. How long would it take for Jack and me to find employment outside the priesthood? "What brought you back to Kansas City?" I said, changing the subject.

"My wife's dad lives here. He's got Alzheimer's. We're taking care of him."

"You're married?"

Mike grinned devilishly. "Why do you think I left the priesthood? Best thing that ever happened to me. Even my former parishioners thought so. We got married at the parish where I was stationed for ten years."

"That's great," I said, envious. Jack and I would never be able to show our faces in any parish where we'd served.

"I even got kids in the deal." Mike pulled his wallet out of his hip pocket and showed me high school graduation photos of a boy and a girl. "They're both in college." He replaced his wallet and looked expectantly at me.

Envious or not, I was glad Mike had applied. "Can you start on Monday?"

AT MIDNIGHT, I climbed out of bed, unable to sleep. Jack was fighting a cold and had decided to spend the night in his own apartment. I felt unsettled all alone on the mattress. I went to the loft overlooking the dark chapel and sat down. The spotlight shone on the golden corpus of the crucifix. Like a flame, the glowing shape mesmerized me.

My thoughts wandered to the interview with Mike. I imagined myself facing a prospective employer across a desk, a man who looked like the archbishop, bald and thin but with a severe expression, scrutinizing me doubtfully as I tried to explain the rich experience I had as an ex-priest. *You do a little of everything,* I heard myself blabbering. *Administration. Counseling. Teaching. You deal with all kinds of people. Communication is a big part of the job. Lots of writing.*

Ex-priest. The word sounded shameful, like *ex-convict.* I imagined my prospective employer's eyebrows raising at the word, his glance asking, *So what did you do to get thrown out? You a child molester or something?*

Why would someone leave such a revered position?

I remembered the thrill of ordination day in St. Peter's Basilica, the hands of the pope himself on my head as I knelt, my eyes fixed on his red shoes. I remembered the spicy aroma of incense wafting around me as the Sistine Chapel choir chanted *Veni, Creator Spiritus.* The moment I'd anticipated for a dozen years had finally come!

Then came congregations who knelt expectantly while I consecrated the wafer, turning bread into Christ for their broken lives. And lost souls pouring out their hearts to me in the confessional. And young parents beaming as I baptized their infants.

Why would someone leave this powerful life? Except to get married. Everyone understood that.

A strange noise that had played at the edge of my consciousness during my reverie suddenly broke through. Someone was in the sacristy. The archbishop always went to bed early and slept like a rock. Jack was the only other person in the building. What was he looking for? I wondered.

I hurried downstairs and crossed the slate floor of the chapel. Genuflecting to the tabernacle, I walked behind the soaring reredos and entered the sacristy. The lights glowed. The wardrobe doors stood open. Albs and chasubles lay in heaps on the floor.

"Jack?" I called.

Down a narrow hallway, a light shone in one of the little chapels where priests used to offer their own private masses. I walked to the room and stopped, in shock. The floor was strewn with vestments—red, green, purple, gold. I picked up a green chasuble. It was ripped from the yoke to the hem. The other vestments were torn, too. Shredded, it seemed, with some kind of blade. A small upholstered chair in the corner of the room had evidently been placed there to facilitate the destruction. Jagged tears in the cushioned seat exposed the foam beneath the fabric.

"What in the hell is going on?" As I turned to look for Jack, the door slammed shut behind me. When I tried to open it, I found it was locked. "Jack. Is that you?" I pounded the door. "What in the hell are you doing?" I peered through the small glass panel but saw no one. "Jack!"

The doors to the small chapels were usually kept wide open, the handles unlocked. The handle of this door might have been inadvertently locked even though the door was open. And the keyhole was on the outside.

Was Jack, messed up as he was, really capable of such senseless destruction? The gun episode had scared me, but at least there had been logic behind the fury. What logic could lay behind these tattered vestments?

No, I couldn't believe Jack had done this. Maybe some troubled kid had broken in to vandalize the place. I would probably find graffiti on the walls somewhere. Or maybe it was Danny, striking out again at Jack.

"All right, you win, Danny!" I shouted, pounding the door. "Let me out."

Pressing my ear to the door, I heard no movement outside.

I scanned the room for a possible means to escape. Two vents in the wall led to the adjacent chapel, but they were much too small for me to pass through. The same rocky panels forming the walls in the large chapel formed the walls here. I considered using the chair, but I doubted its usefulness in battering through the barrier. Even if I could break through the rocks, it would take forever and destroy the wall. No, I might as well resign myself to this prison until the archbishop came down at six to say his morning prayers.

Sitting in the chair, I stared at the door, listening for noise in the sacristy, imagining someone wielding a knife out there. Eventually I relaxed. The culprit must have fled. Shaping a bed out of the chasubles, I kicked off my shoes, extinguished the light, and stretched out on the soft vestments. For a long time, my gaze remained fixed on the glass panel. But finally I drifted off.

SEVERAL HOURS LATER, a noise in the sacristy woke me up. I sprang to my feet and pounded the door. "Archbishop, is that you? Open the door."

The archbishop's puzzled eyes appeared in the window and the door opened.

"What happened?" he said, glancing in alarm at the pile of vestments. "Have you been in here all night?"

As I filled the archbishop in, his brow wrinkled in concern. "Who would do such a thing?"

I shrugged. "I'll look around the building. To see where they broke in."

"We should call the police," the archbishop said.

"I'll do it, Archbishop. Go ahead and say your morning prayers."

I inspected the front doors of the building and the windows in the corridors around the main chapel. Nothing was disturbed. But in the connecting corridor leading to the recreation building, I found a window with an open latch. When I had checked the windows before I went to bed, as usual, I must have overlooked this one. Was it the point of entry?

In the predawn darkness, it was difficult to inspect the shrubbery for signs of an intruder, and I figured I'd leave that to the police and went to my office and called them. Two officers showed up. They poked around for a while and took down some information before leaving.

An hour later, I found myself checking Jack's reaction as I told him about the break-in. We were in the locker room by the pool, preparing to swim laps. Naked, a towel around his muscular neck, Jack listened attentively on a bench, looking surprised. I felt foolish for ever suspecting him of the crime.

"I think it was Danny," I said, stripping off my jeans. "He was pretty pissed at you. If he's unstable . . ." I knew there was no reason to elaborate. Jack obviously knew better than I did the workings of Danny's mind.

But if he suspected anything, he kept it to himself. Thinking over my observation, he shrugged. "Who knows?"

AFTER LUNCH, I was at my desk when Danny walked into the office, unannounced. I shot to my feet.

"What's the matter, Father?" Danny grinned. Dressed in a black leather jacket and black jeans, he looked like a tough biker.

"Are you here to confess something?" I said, fuming.

Danny's smile disappeared. "I'm not the one with something to confess. I told you that."

"You weren't here last night?"

"Why would I be?" Danny said, staring hatefully. "I was at the restaurant. Working."

"After work."

"I don't know what you're talking about, Father."

"All right," I conceded. Maybe he wasn't the culprit. And if he was, my accusations would clearly not prompt a confession. "How can I help you?"

"Can I sit down?"

Reluctantly, I gestured to the sofa. He removed his jacket and took a seat. I came around the desk and stood facing him.

"Could you shut the door?" Danny said.

"I'd rather leave it open."

He sat back sullenly and folded his arms.

"I'll be honest with you, Danny. I think you're lying about Father Canston. I've told the archbishop what you said. He doesn't believe you either. So, that's the end of it. You need to stay away from Father Canston. And you need to stay away from here. If I see you here, I'm going to call the police."

Danny glared at me. "Father Jack fucked me!" he shouted.

I glanced nervously toward the hallway. Debbie was in her office. So were Alberta and Fran. And the diocesan chancellor was working on annulment cases in an office down the hall. I got up and shut the door. I remained standing, ready to usher Danny out as soon as possible.

Danny studied me with satisfaction. "You're lying about the archbishop," he said.

"I'm telling you, this is over."

"He'd be at my door in a minute if he knew. He's got orders from the Vatican now to go after the *maricones*."

"What do you want?"

"I want you to listen to me, Father."

"I have listened to you."

"Please, Father," Danny said, his tone softening. "Sit down, and just listen to me."

I knew I had no choice, and I obeyed.

Danny settled back on the couch, his legs spread, his square hands on thighs. "My mother's from a little village near Playa del Carmen. A big family. Her father worked in the city at a hotel. He supervised the cleaning staff. Got Mama a job there. A man staying in one of the rooms raped her. An American businessman. Mama's father cut him up bad. He got fired, couldn't find no work. He sent Mama and two of my uncles to live with his brother's family up here. She met my father. They fell in love. Got married. Had four children. My father opened the restaurant. Everybody loved him. Everybody was his friend."

"So he died?" I said, without pity.

"Fucking cancer, Father. We prayed. On our knees around his bed." Danny's eyes filled and he choked up. "Mama lit candles at church. She told us God would save him if we just kept praying. And you know what? God didn't save him. So, I said to hell with God. I got tough. Hung out with a gang. We stole a car. They stuck us all in BIS. The Boys' Industrial School." Danny pronounced the name of the reformatory with mock awe. "What a joke. You could get whatever shit you wanted there. Pot. Crack. Whatever."

I said nothing, waiting for him to finish and leave.

"The Virgin saved me." He pulled up the sleeve of his sweatshirt to expose the image on his forearm. "I had a dream about her. She was holding my father in her arms. Like that statue in Rome or somewhere. Only the Virgin was nursing him, like a baby. You think that's gross?"

I shrugged.

"Some people do. But she's our holy mother right? She says to me, 'I'll take care of him if you're good.'" Danny had been straining forward, his dark eyes watching for my reaction. Now that his story was finished, he leaned back and crossed his arms.

"Why are you telling me this?" I said, suspicious of his motives for appealing to my sympathy.

"So you'll understand."

"Understand what?"

"Why I've got to stay straight. Why I need a spiritual director."

"All right. I understand."

"And I want you to be the one."

Incredulous, I shook my head. "I'm not going to be your spiritual director, Danny." I stood up. "Look, you need to go. I've got other appointments."

"You don't do it, I tell the archbishop about Father Jack." Danny stared coolly at me.

"What do you want from me?" I snapped.

"And I tell him about the two of you. You're *maricones.* Who fucks who?"

A wave of heat rushed into my face.

"I'm not stupid, you know, Father." Danny grinned. "So, will you do it?"

"No."

Danny chuckled. He got up, grabbing his coat, and approached me. "You will." He patted my chest and kissed me on the cheek, before moving to the door.

"Did you break in last night?" I called after him. "Did you break in and tear up the vestments?"

"I told you no, Father. I'm not a liar." Danny left without another word.

I stood there, frozen on the spot, not knowing how to respond. But after a moment, I started to go after Danny. I'd make it clear that no one was going to blackmail me. Especially a kid half my age. But before I could get out of the room, Alberta showed up, blocking the door. She stared at me, concerned.

"What was that all about?" she said.

"He threatened me."

She stepped in and shut the door. "What do you mean?"

I told her about Danny's proposal and his threat. "He's lying," I said. "The archbishop would never believe him. I'll tell him that Danny's the one who broke into the sacristy and tore up the vestments. The archbishop will see that he's demented."

"No, no, no." Alberta folded her arms and shook her head angrily. "You dismiss this, you'll be sorry."

"Sorry about what?" I said. "That I believed Jack instead of a disturbed kid? He's pissed at Jack. That's all. He knows exactly how to do him the most damage."

"Chris," she pleaded. She closed the door and sat on the couch. "Come here." She patted the couch. "Sit down."

"I don't want a lecture."

"Please. Sit down."

Resentful, I sat in an armchair instead of the couch.

"It's out of your control," she said. "You didn't bring this on. You didn't ask Jack to come back here with whatever baggage he's carrying. His problems aren't your problems."

"Would you say that if Jack were a woman I was engaged to? I don't think so. I think you'd tell me to help her. To defend her against malicious attacks."

Alberta narrowed her eyes at me. "Don't play the homophobia card with me. You know that you and Jack are not engaged in any way. You're not free to be. Your relationship is a big ol' secret."

"So what? You don't just move from priesthood to married life like that." I snapped my fingers. "I know we've got decisions to make. Why can't you just support me?"

"Support!" Alberta snorted. "Support means telling you the truth, whether you want to hear it or not."

"And how did you get the corner on the truth market?"

"Please, Chris! Do you really think I get a kick out of causing you grief? I'm looking out for you, and you know it."

"No, I don't. You're looking out for the church or the diocese or my holy vocation. You haven't even heard *me.* What *I* want."

Alberta looked indignant. "Well, excuse me," she said, raising her hands in mock apology. "I thought you *wanted* to do the right thing."

"So there's nothing really to think about is there? The right thing is a vow I made twenty years ago, before I even knew myself."

Alberta shook her head. "That's not what I'm saying. Of course you have to listen to your heart. But you have to make decisions with your eyes open."

I turned away, not wanting to hear this.

"Something's not right with Jack. You know it yourself. You can't fix him. I'm not saying this kid is telling the truth."

"He's not, Alberta," I lied, shamelessly. "And he's got the power to cause Jack and me a lot of misery. We don't have jobs lined up or a place to go. And, yes, Jack's gotta get better. *Before* he makes a drastic change in his life."

"I could talk to him."

"No!" The thought horrified me. Jack would explode if he knew that I'd told Alberta about his problems. "Let me handle this."

Alberta stared at me doubtfully but made no rebuttal.

13

FOR THE REST of the day, I tried to figure out what to do. I hated keeping Danny's visit a secret from Jack, but telling him could send him over the edge. And, of course, I would never go to the police as I'd threatened to do. The truth about Jack and me would come out. My deepest fear was that exposure would ruin everything for us. Instead of driving Jack into my arms, it would make him run away from me. He might even try to kill himself again.

That evening I did my best to hide my worries from Jack. During dinner, I avoided any topic that could bring up Danny's name. Afterward, I worked in my office until late. When I passed Jack's door on the way to my apartment, I knocked gently. When he didn't answer, I was relieved. He'd probably gone to bed early, worn out by his cold.

It took me a long time to fall asleep, and not long after I did, I got a phone call from an old parishioner in Lawrence, Tom Nguyen, whose wife was dying. He asked me to come to their house. I got up and dressed and drove all the way to Lawrence.

At three in the morning, the streets in the Nguyens' neighborhood were empty. Cold rain sprinkled the windshield as I pulled up in front of their big four-square house with gables. I'd spent many summer evenings on the front porch with the Nguyen family when I was pastor at Holy Angels. Meagan Nguyen had developed breast cancer just before I'd left the parish. The disease had steadily advanced despite chemotherapy and radiation. Now, she had come to the end of her suffering.

Tom greeted me at the door, a slight man, gray at the temples. Even in this tragic moment, he smiled graciously and embraced me. "Sorry to get you out of bed, Father."

I squeezed his arm. "Is Meagan still conscious?"

"In and out. Janey said she'll go anytime now."

I'd met Janey, the hearty, efficient nurse from the hospice. She'd supported the family's decision to let Meagan die at home, even though it meant much more work and stress for all of them.

In the den, the family was gathered around a hospital bed. A soothing, ethereal Enya chant played over the sound system. Photo albums were open on the coffee table next to a vase of yellow daisies. The Nguyens' curly-haired mut jogged over and leaped up on my legs.

"Hey, Oscar!" I petted the dog.

"Hi, Father." The teenaged girl who embraced me was tall and striking, with intelligent eyes.

"God, Amelia," I said. "You've grown!"

Amelia's eyes welled up. "Father!" she blurted, breaking down.

I hugged her.

The Nguyens' married son, Mark, stood at the bed with his pregnant wife, along with Tom's parents and Janey, who patted me on the back. Meagan's parents were both dead.

In one short month since my last visit, Meagan had wasted to nothing. Her eyes were sunken, and her prominent skull threatened to tear through her jaundiced skin. Her beautiful, silky hair was gone. The feeding tube had been removed per instructions she'd written earlier. Her kidneys had ceased to function.

I lit Meagan's baptismal candle, a possession she'd prized her whole life. I took my white stole out of my briefcase and slipped it around my neck. As I read the prayers and anointed Meagan's forehead, lips, and hands, Mark sobbed. His white-haired parents comforted him.

When I finished the ritual, I kissed Meagan on the head. "May the angels come to meet you," I whispered.

The end came within an hour. I waited with the family for the men from the mortuary to come for the body. Amelia showed me pictures in the photo album, every now and then glancing at the still figure on the bed, as though maybe she'd open her eyes for just another minute.

When the morticians arrived, the family became agitated, as though the strange men collecting Meagan were cruelly wrenching her away from them. Amelia became hysterical. Tom's daughter-in-law fainted, and Janey attended to her. I stayed until everyone had calmed.

"Thank you, Father," Tom said at the door, choked with emotion. "You brought God with you." He embraced me.

As I drove home, I felt the deep satisfaction of a shepherd who'd cared for his sheep. And suddenly I felt I was crazy to consider leaving such a life. How could I do it? How could Jack? Maybe Alberta was right. I was expecting the impossible—Jack all cured and the two of us living happily ever after in the suburbs. I had to keep Danny quiet. I had to do what he wanted, or Jack and I would be cast out of paradise.

But back in my apartment, when I picked up the phone to call Danny, I couldn't go through with it. I couldn't stand the thought of being at his beck and call. I put down the phone and went to bed.

I slept all morning. When I got to my office at one o' clock, I found two messages from Danny, ordering me to call him. I tried to pick up the phone and punch in his number, but I couldn't.

During the course of the afternoon, I looked fondly at the photos the Nguyen family had given me. I hung them in magnetic frames on the file cabinet, where I could see them from my desk. I dusted my ordination certificate on the wall and washed the pottery chalice and communion plate I kept displayed on a shelf—ordination gifts from my first parish.

I called to check on Tom. Then I called Lauren, the teenager who had come out to me. She thanked me effusively for counseling her. She'd joined a lesbian volleyball team. Buoyed by the sense of my own gentle authority, I even called my mother and listened patiently to a litany of her ailments.

While I worked steadily on a sermon for an upcoming retreat mass at St. John's, my phone rang. I was afraid it was Danny, so I didn't answer. But when I played back the message, I was relieved. It was from Mark Andersen, the guy with the shaved head who'd come to my office with his partner Barry, asking me to conduct their wedding. I called him back.

"How's it hanging, Father?" Mark said in his brassy voice.

"Great," I lied, laughing.

"Barry and I bought a new house. Wanted to invite you to our housewarming Saturday night. Nothing fancy. Just a few friends."

"This Saturday?" I searched my mind for an excuse. Jack wasn't ready for a gay party, and I was too chicken to go alone.

"Hey, we won't take no for an answer, Padre. You gotta at least make an appearance."

Somehow this seemed like a moment of truth, facing myself and the question of my future with Jack. "Is it okay if I bring a friend?" I said.

"Sure," Mark said. "The more the merrier."

"Actually, he's more than a friend. He's my boyfriend."

"Father! I'm appalled," Mark exclaimed with mock horror. Then he chuckled. "We can't wait to meet him."

JACK DIDN'T BLINK an eye when I asked him to go to the party that night while we watched TV. "Why not?" he said, with a calculated nonchalance, his eyes still on the screen. He seemed to sense that it was important to me and that it was some kind of test that he could endure.

"They know about us. That we're not just friends." I had to be sure he understood what he was getting himself into.

He didn't respond for a moment, and I held my breath. Finally, he shrugged. "All right," he said with the same studied indifference. "Why not?"

I was pleasantly surprised by his response, unenthusiastic or not. And I was frightened. The party would be our first public moment as a couple. I fretted about it all week.

ON SATURDAY NIGHT in Jack's living room, I waited nervously while he showered. My palms were damp. I felt hot in my sweater. I got up, opened the window, and inhaled the cold air.

Jack entered the living room in his briefs, drying his hair with a towel. "It's freezing in here," he said testily, slamming the window shut and lighting a cigarette.

"If you don't wanna go . . ." I snapped.

"I said I'd go, didn't I?" Jack shot back, returning to his bedroom.

God, please get us through this night, I prayed.

On the drive to Mark and Barry's, Jack smoked four cigarettes. When we arrived at their house, a cozy bungalow, he lit another. We silently processed through the paper-bag luminarias glowing on each side of the sidewalk and rang the doorbell, even though the oak door was open and we could see people laughing through the glass storm door.

A bearded man holding a glass of wine opened the door. "Come on in," he said. "Welcome to the party."

A dozen people filled the softly lit living room. An attractive young couple sat on the sofa, the man's arm around the woman. A small group of men chatted animatedly by the fireplace. Two middle-aged women stood by the piano and sang show tunes while a chubby man played. More people gathered in the dining room. Mark appeared in a white silk shirt with a banded collar.

"Chris! Welcome!" Mark embraced me. "This must be Jack." He stuck out his hand.

Looking uncomfortable, Jack shook Mark's hand.

"What would you like to drink?" Mark said. He ran through a list of beverages and went to the kitchen to get us the beers we'd requested.

"You told him about us?" Jack said.

"Why wouldn't I? Don't worry. He's not going to report us to the celibacy police."

Jack downed his beer quickly while I chatted with Barry, who'd emerged from the kitchen, then retrieved another and drank it self-consciously under the frequent, admiring glances of the group by the fireplace.

On their way to refreshments in the dining room, the young couple who'd been sitting on the sofa introduced themselves as Melinda and Drew. They were friendly and unpretentious despite their good looks and quirky, avant-garde clothes.

"That's a beautiful necklace," I said to Melinda, touching the band of lapis lazuli around her throat.

"Thank you. *I* made it," she boasted.

"She makes cosmetics, too," Drew said, proudly. He wore tortoiseshell horn-rimmed glasses. "And she sells them."

"I'm impressed," I said. "I wondered why your skin glowed."

Melinda smiled appreciatively. "What do you guys do?" she said.

Jack threw me a warning glance and swallowed his beer.

"Counseling," I answered. At least it was partially true.

Through more introductions and small talk, Jack continued to drink. Instead of relaxing him, the alcohol made him surly and even quieter. He gave clipped answers to questions and stared around the room. People began addressing me only. I tried to make up for his rudeness by being doubly friendly, and I was getting exhausted. I was glad when Jack finally announced he wanted to go.

"I'll go tell Mark and Barry good-bye," I said.

As I turned to the piano where our hosts and several guests were singing, a familiar face at the door brought me to a dead halt. It was Danny, in his black leather jacket and black jeans. I went to the door and confronted him. "What are you doing here?"

"I followed you." Danny grinned. "Cool house." Danny pushed past me, approaching Jack.

I pursued him.

Jack looked furious.

"What are you doing here, Father? With a bunch of fags." He glanced at the man at the piano, crooning in falsetto.

"Let's go," Jack said to me.

"Father Chris invited me," Danny blurted.

"He's lying," I said.

Danny laughed. "He's my new spiritual director."

Jack threw me a confused look.

"I'm not," I said. "He's lying."

"Hey everybody," Danny shouted. "These are two priests of God."

Heads turned. People stopped singing. Then the music stopped. When Danny repeated his cry, Jack grabbed him by the throat and pushed him against the wall, holding him there. Danny's face reddened and his eyes widened, but he didn't fight back. He glared at Jack, almost as though he dared him to kill him. And Jack, his jaw clenched and his face thrust in Danny's, seemed ready to oblige him.

For a moment, the alarm of seeing Jack turn into the same savage I had witnessed at the drive-in paralyzed me. Then I moved into action, grabbing Jack by the arm.

"Let him go," I whispered, my heart racing.

Jack paid me no attention, continuing his hold on Danny.

Finally, Mark rushed over and pried the two apart.

"Some priest!" Danny said scornfully, rubbing his throat. "First he tries to put the moves on me. Then he tries to choke me to death."

The silence in the room bore down on me like a weight. "I'm so sorry, Mark," I said.

Mark shook his head as though no apology were needed. "Play, play, play!" he implored the piano player.

The music and talking resumed, though eyes kept darting to the scene. Looking concerned, Barry approached us and stood by Mark.

"You come near me again, I'll kill you," Jack said to Danny. His face was still pale with rage. Pushing past Danny, he left the house.

Through the storm door, I watched him head to the truck.

Danny smiled triumphantly at me.

"Why are you doing this?" I said.

"You know, Father."

"I'm going to have to ask you to leave," Mark said to him.

Danny eyed him with contempt. Then he sauntered out without another word.

"God, I'm sorry, Mark," I said. "I had no idea that he followed us here." I didn't bring up Jack's behavior. I was too mortified. I knew that Mark and Barry must have been thinking I was involved with a madman.

"Who is he?" Barry said.

"Long story," I answered evasively. "Guess I'm off your guest list from now on."

"Hey, Chris," Mark said, patting my back reassuringly. "Queens love a little drama."

As we drove back to St. John's, Jack said nothing. He just fingered his rosary, staring at the road. I watched him, searching for something reassuring in his stony gaze. He'd terrified me a second time, and I wondered how long it would be before he lost control again. On both occasions, being branded a faggot had triggered the rage. And tonight he'd chafed in a room where everyone knew what he was. Maybe he'd chafed all the more because others in the room shared his nature, and once you start associating with others like you, the whole world knows what you are.

In that moment, staring at him in the dark truck, I had to face the devastating truth.

"This isn't going to work, is it?" I said quietly. "My big fantasy. You and me in a cozy house full of our friends."

I might as well have been talking to myself. Jack was oblivious to the question.

"Why didn't you tell me he came to your office?" he said. "Debbie told me."

"He just showed up. I warned him to stay away."

Jack threw me an accusatory glance. "It didn't work." He switched on the radio and turned it up loud.

So, that was it, I thought. End of conversation.

We rode in silence, but when we got home Jack apologized. He kissed me and asked me to forgive him for losing control. I did forgive him. I even let him make love to me. But afterward, as I lay next to him, I quietly pondered the hard facts. We were not like Mark and Barry. We might never be.

Jack Canston's Journal

February 4

The shrinks at the hospital preached about *personal identity*. Personal identity this, personal identity that. I can see that bug-eyed shrink, Walters, looking up from his notebook through his horn-rims: "This is a clear case of a personal identity crisis, Mr. Canston. Look at it as a window of opportunity."

Bullshit! Obsession with personal identity is the fucking problem with the world. What matters except your will, O God? What matters except obedience to your laws? Not human laws! Not the little doctrines about celibacy or sexuality dreamed up after the church's true formative years. After the scriptural canon was established! They don't matter. They don't. They don't. I've always believed that. They're not worth one crumb of the consecrated host, which is Truth made flesh. His body, given up for us.

Part Three

THE RESCUE

In justice shall you be established,
far from the fear of oppression,
where destruction cannot come near you.
Should there be any attack,
it shall not be of my making;
whoever attacks you shall fall before you.

—ISAIAH 54: 13–14

14

THE NEXT MORNING at the bathroom mirror, as I dabbed a shaving cut on my throat with toilet paper, the truth I'd glimpsed the night before suddenly loomed before me, bright and indisputable: everything had to be different. I had to face the facts about Jack and about myself. I couldn't cure him. I couldn't change him. And unless I stopped living in a dream world, I'd be stuck in the mud along with him. It was time to tell the truth. It was time to act. If I had some balls, I could help Jack, even if I couldn't cure him. I could help myself. It was time to confront the demons. Starting with Danny Flores.

THE SUN HAD climbed above the bare trees when I pulled up in front of Danny's little house. With a sense of purpose, I jumped out of the car and marched to the front door. I hadn't given

Danny any notice. A surprise attack was the best way to handle someone so rash he might do something like call the media to announce that a priest of the archdiocese had sexually assaulted him.

Mrs. Flores showed up at the door after my relentless knocking and ringing the bell. Her hair was disheveled and her eyes puffy. She pulled her terrycloth bathrobe around herself and opened the storm door.

"Hello, Mrs. Flores," I said. "I have to talk to Danny."

She put her hand to her chest in alarm. "Did he do something again?"

"Yes," I said without hesitating. "I need to talk to him right away."

"He's in bed. Come in."

I waited in the tight, dark living room while she went to get her son. A little spotlight illumined the Virgin's photo on the television.

Mrs. Flores returned, shaking her head. "It's no good, Father. He had too much to drink. I can't wake him up."

I half-considered dragging him out of bed anyway but realized that it would do no good if he was incoherent. The confrontation would have to wait. "Does he drink a lot?" I said.

She shrugged helplessly and her eyes welled up.

"Does he go out with friends?" I knew this was wishful thinking—to imagine he actually had someone else to think about other than Jack and me.

"I don't know, Father. He doesn't tell me nothing. Sometimes he leaves after the restaurant closes and doesn't come home until morning. I've told him not to get in trouble again. What should I do?"

"There's nothing you can do," I said, feeling sorry for her. "I'll talk to him later."

"I'll have him call you when he gets up," she said.

"No!" I didn't want a ranting phone call from him. "Please don't tell him anything. Just pray for him, and let me take care of it."

There was no guarantee that Mrs. Flores would cooperate, but she did look relieved to be absolved of responsibility.

As I made my way to the door she called after me imploringly.

"The Virgin won't stop protecting him, will she? If I keep praying?"

"She won't stop," I said, glancing back. "Everything will be all right."

I knew there was nothing I could do for now but get in the car and drive away. And that's what I did, but I was determined not to give up. Maybe I could corner Danny at church when he was sober and on his best behavior.

The visit made me think of my own mother, and while I was in town I stopped to see her. As she rolled out a pie crust on the kitchen counter, she brought up the rumors going around about Eddie's dark secret.

"How can they say that?" she said, glancing up at me at the table.

"Who cares what they say? Eddie's dead."

"Mrs. Gerhardt cares! Eddie's good name is being dragged through the mud. If the people spreading this gossip had known Edward when he was a boy—he was so polite and funny."

"Right, Mom," I said, sarcastically. "That would really convince them."

She frowned and pushed up her glasses. "Well, knowing people makes a difference."

"Mom," I suddenly said, "I did know Eddie. He was gay."

When she stared up at me as though the wind had been knocked out of her, I saw the moment had come. I couldn't reveal the truth about Eddie and keep myself hidden. As much as I dreaded her reaction, I added, "And I'm gay, too."

For a minute she seemed not to have heard me. She sadly shook her head, as if she was still thinking about Eddie, and went back to her rolling. Then she suddenly stopped and looked up at me, her mouth twisted and her eyes batting as if she was half annoyed and half fighting tears. She finally said, "Well, that doesn't matter if you're a priest."

"It does to me."

She looked confused. Then she started trembling and swiping at tears. When I got up and hugged her, she started to cry, muttering over and over, "Why did you tell me?"

I thought she would want to talk after she calmed down, but she didn't. When I finally asked her if she had any questions, she shrugged despondently and said she had wash to do. I could see that I'd hurt her profoundly, and she had no use for me at the moment. So I left, feeling awful about upsetting her but not regretting what I'd done.

One step forward, two steps back. Isn't that what they say? The adage proved true for me that day. When I got back to St. John's, a cryptic e-mail message from the archbishop was waiting for me: "Please come to my office immediately upon receiving this." The abrupt note was unlike the archbishop's usual messages, which always included a salutation and signature, no matter how perfunctory the communication.

Nervous, I proceeded to the archbishop's office. The door was open. I rapped on it and stepped in to find the archbishop staring out his window, his hands clasped behind his back. He turned and gestured for me to have a seat. Then he removed his black suit jacket from the back of his desk chair and slipped it on, straightening his studded cuffs as though to prepare for official business.

After he closed the door and took a seat, the archbishop cleared his throat and gazed gravely at me. "I've received a disturbing report about you, Chris," he said. "It's a very serious matter."

My thoughts immediately went to Danny. I figured he'd carried out his threat and told the archbishop, probably in a rage-muddled phone call after the scene at Barry and Mark's. The archbishop confirmed my fears, coming right to the point.

"I've learned that you are having homosexual relations with Father Canston," he said. "Is this true?"

"Who told you that? If it was Danny Flores—"

The archbishop raised his hand to interrupt me. "It doesn't matter. I'm asking you now."

"But it does matter, Archbishop. Danny is unstable. He's taking advantage of the Vatican mandate to strike out at Jack and me. I think he's the one responsible for the ruined vestments."

The archbishop frowned. "Why should anyone want to strike out at two priests?"

"He spent several years at BIS. He's been on drugs. He resents authority figures. Jack has been trying to help him."

The archbishop pondered the information, then appeared to brush it aside. "Please answer my question," he persisted. "Are you in an illicit relationship with Father Canston?"

I almost laughed at the term. The archbishop made our love sound like incest. "What if I were?" I said.

"Then I would have no choice but to dismiss you from your position at St. John's and begin procedures for your removal from ministry altogether."

"You're saying that an affair is cause for kicking someone out of the priesthood?" I said indignantly. "Offhand, I can name five priests in the diocese who've received a slap on the wrist for affairs."

"I'm addressing the issue of homosexual affairs."

"What's the difference?"

"Chris, you know what the difference is. Especially now that the Catholic Church across the country is in the middle of a sex-abuse scandal. Dioceses are paying millions of dollars in damages to victims abused as children by our own priests."

"Most pedophiles are heterosexuals!" I protested, incensed by his implication that gay men were all sexual predators. "There are studies of this."

"Be that as it may. People in the pews don't make such distinctions."

"Then we should educate them." I knew how ludicrous the suggestion was even as I made it. The idea of the archbishop going to bat for his queer priests!

"I'm waiting," the archbishop said solemnly.

"No," I said stubbornly. "It's not true." My tone dared the archbishop to challenge me, despite his clear disbelief. I figured he deserved to be put in this awkward position: either he had to risk having me publicly defend myself in a troubled diocese or he had to accept my claim and rationalize that he'd done his duty to ask. I almost hoped he would choose the first option and force me—and Jack—to go public with our relationship and end the shameful hiding.

But he chose the safer route. "Very well," he said. "That's all I wanted to know. But I hope that you and Father Canston will keep in mind how dangerous even appearances can be."

"We'll do that, Archbishop."

Back in my bedroom, cogs spun in my head as I changed into sweats. My racing thoughts seemed to generate heat that rushed through me. If I didn't release it, I would explode.

Outside, my breath smoked in the damp cold. I sprinted across the field to the road and flew down the first hill and up the next. I ran hard all the way to the park. Then I slackened my pace, my strides even, my body drawing on energy I'd gained rather than lost in the sprint.

Stay hidden. Stay closeted. That's all that is asked of you. The archbishop's reasonable voice sounded in my mind, as I imagined the words he most wanted to speak. *Silence has worked for centuries. It has saved the church with no real sacrifice to you. You're the offender, after all. And an offender who reaps the benefits of this sacred institution of men.*

"Fuck you, Koch!" I shouted. "Fuck your goddamned silence!"

My sneakers pounded the paved road that wound through the park. I picked up speed, tears streaming down my face. When I exited the park and came to the spot where Jack and I had found the dead dog, I stopped, my chest heaving.

Why had Jack ever come back to me—damaged as he was, too damaged to give me what I needed? What I thought had been a blessing—was it really a curse?

I walked the rest of the way to St. John's. At the rear of the buildings, I stared up at Jack's window. My longing for him ripped into me like a steel blade. No, I decided, he wasn't a curse. How could love be a curse, no matter how much pain it caused?

After I showered, I ate a sandwich in the kitchen, checked on a project that Debbie was doing for me in the office, and returned to my apartment, deciding to take the rest of the day off. I sat quietly on the sofa, watching the fish dart through the aquarium plants, thinking about the confrontation with the archbishop. I was glad that Danny had done his worst. He had no more cards to play, unless he really did approach the media and scare the archbishop into defrocking Jack and me to avoid a scandal. But what did it matter? Sooner or later Koch had to know the truth. At least about me. I had to tell him. Before I did, however, I owed it to Jack to let him know my plans.

I decided to give it to him straight that night at dinner. The archbishop was attending a parish anniversary celebration, so he would be out of the way and Jack and I could have the dining room to ourselves. To put him in a good mood, I made his favorite meal: steak and baked potatoes. I also pulled out a bottle of merlot from a stock of wine in the pantry. But I didn't want to give him the wrong idea, that this was a prelude to a romantic evening, so I set the table with our everyday cotton napkins and the plain china stacked in the kitchen.

I'd left him a note in his apartment, so when he got home at six-thirty he came to the kitchen still in his clerical shirt, the tab in his pocket, and with a new short haircut. As he helped me carry the food into the dining room, he seemed to be in a good mood. He'd gone to sleep the night before reassured of my forgiveness and probably wiping from his mind the ugly scene at Mark and Barry's. I'd never met someone as proficient as Jack at blocking out unpleasant things—compartmentalizing—although the trauma he'd gone through because of Ben's death had shaken that ability. Of course, the trauma also explained his blowups. I'd gotten used to treating him gingerly, so I was nervous now. But it was time to push him—and before he'd had too much wine.

So we'd only taken a few bites of our meal when I told him about the archbishop's question. He'd been joking about his new haircut making him look like a marine—which it did, in a way—and suddenly his smile vanished. He chewed his steak angrily and glared across the table at me as though he expected to hear I'd confessed everything. When I told him how I'd answered the archbishop, he looked relieved and nodded with approval.

"I'll put a stop to this," he said, sipping his wine. "I'll talk to Danny tomorrow."

I couldn't believe what I was hearing. "No. Are you crazy? You've done enough. Besides, Danny can't do any more damage."

Jack seemed ready to protest but then thought better of it, as though unwilling to test my patience. His restraint gave me a sense of satisfaction in my own moral authority and a sense of hope that he really could get past his anger and grief over Ben's death. I even dared to push him further.

"Maybe Danny has done his worst with the archbishop," I said. "But he could run to the media and stir up a scandal. Koch might get rid of us whether he defended us or not."

Jack frowned in alarm. "You think so?" Then he dismissed the idea with a shake of his head. "No, the archbishop will go to bat for his priests." He confidently dug into his baked potato with a fork and shoveled it into his mouth.

But I pressed him. "He doesn't really believe me, Jack. He wouldn't go to bat for us. I promise you."

"What do you mean, he doesn't believe you?"

"I mean, he asked me for the truth out of a sense of duty. And he prayed that I would say what he wanted to hear, whether it was true or not. I could tell."

Jack's angry scowl returned. He leaned forward on his elbows. "You didn't even try to sound convincing?"

"No, I didn't." I slammed down my fork. "Because I don't like lying. I'm ashamed of myself for doing it. And I don't intend to keep it up."

Jack shoved his chair away from the table and shot to his feet. Clenching his jaw, the same frightening fury in his eyes that I'd witnessed when he throttled Danny, he picked up his glass and squeezed it. I cringed, waiting for it to shatter in his hand. But he got hold of himself, relaxing his grip and setting the glass softly on the table. His anger melting away, he now he stared helplessly at me. "Please don't do it, Chris," he said softly. "Don't tell him about us."

As he begged me, I felt so much tenderness for him that I might have promised anything. But I managed to keep my resolution. "I won't tell about us," I said. "Not unless you agree to it. But I will tell him about me. I told my mother today. And it felt good."

Jack shook his head and said bitterly, "It won't feel good when you tell him. You'll lose everything."

"I don't want priesthood at this price. Do you? You said you were willing to leave."

"Where am I gonna go?" he snorted. "Like this?" He stretched his big hands toward his chest as if to indicate the mess inside of him.

I saw this admission as a reason for hope, as an opportunity, and I grabbed it. "You can get over Ben's death, Jack. You can. You can put the pieces back together. But you need help. Professional help. You're not in a position to decide anything until you get it."

He smirked at me as though my advice showed I knew nothing, or nothing about him. "I've had professional help," he said. "Remember?" He sat back down and leaned back in his chair.

"In a state hospital. After a breakdown." I was determined to state the facts, not to treat him as something fragile and dangerous. "It's time for normal counseling. Please."

"Okay," he said, wearily. "I'll get help."

"When?" I pressed.

"I'll call someone first thing tomorrow." He sat quietly for a moment, then reached across the table and took my hand. "You know, even if we leave the priesthood, we're priests forever. That's what the ordination rite says, 'You are a priest forever, according to the order of Melchisadek.'"

His strange smile unsettled me. Only half-joking, he seemed to be saying that there was no escape from our destiny. Our holy vocation would haunt us even if we never set foot within the door of another Catholic church for the rest of our lives.

15

IN THE FIRST light of dawn, Jack sat on the edge of the bed, smoking a cigarette, his smooth back to me. Meaty flesh padded his shoulder blades, and I wanted to trace the gentle valley between them with my hand and run my fingers down under the waistband of his briefs. He perched on the mattress like a big child who relied on my protection, but I reminded myself that, for all my tenderness, I couldn't control him. Everything was up to him. It was his life.

That morning, he left for Santa Rosa's at seven-thirty. I picked up the paper from the front of the main building and carried it to the kitchen, where I made coffee and toast and thumbed through the pages. When I came to an article about the new Vatican mandate, it irritated me too much to read it. I pitched the paper and went to my apartment to look at a course catalog I'd gotten in the mail from the University of Kansas. I'd marked the pages outlining the degree program in counseling. As I sat at the desk, reading the course descriptions, my head spun:

Theories of Child Counseling, Counseling in Community Settings, Career Counseling, Couples Counseling. Which area did I want to specialize in? And did I really want to spend three years in school just so I could do what I'd been doing for fifteen years?

But I had to make a living somehow if I left the priesthood. And my master's degree in divinity wouldn't put food on the table.

I read through the pages on financial aid, my mind swimming with practical questions: Where would I live? How would I make my car payments—and insurance? I knew Jack was in no position to think of these things. I'd need to leave first and prepare the way until he could think clearly and make his own decisions.

When the phone rang, I hoped it was Jack. I wanted to tell him what I was doing, to get him used to the idea that we had to make plans. But when I answered it, no one spoke.

"Jack?" I said.

In the silence that followed, my gaze fell on a stack of business cards on my desk. An idea had crossed my mind after the last mysterious call, when I remembered that I'd given my card to someone I almost dreaded to hear from. That idea returned now.

"George?" I said. "Is this George Madson?"

I could hear someone breathing, but no response preceded the click and dial tone.

In my office, as I worked on my monthly column for the *Mustard Seed*, the uncomfortable presentiment about George lingered in the back of my mind. George worked for Eddie. He probably saw Eddie nearly every day. I'd felt he was hiding something. What was it? I kept seeing his blue eyes resenting me for probing him about Eddie, and I kept wondering if the resentment came because he felt blamed or because he felt forced to confess something I probably wouldn't believe. Had I just dismissed my suspicions that day because I couldn't bear the thought that Eddie could have hurt George? Because I couldn't bring myself to believe such a thing? I still didn't believe it now. But I had a duty to find out the truth.

After lunch, I finally pulled out my Topeka phone book and called the number I found for Madson on Tyler Street, where St. Mary's was located. Mrs. Madson answered.

"This is Father Seib," I said. "I'm the administrator at the diocesan center."

"Yes, Father. You were at Father Edward's funeral."

"That's right. I was at St. Mary's not too long ago. I met your son, George. He was shoveling snow."

"I saw you out the window," she said. "I'm glad you talked to George. He's been down about Father Edward. I've tried to talk to him, but he won't open up."

"I noticed he was taking it hard. I told him to give me a call whenever he wanted to talk. But he hasn't taken me up on my offer. I just thought I'd check on him."

"That's so nice of you, Father."

"Is he there now?"

"No. He's at a basketball game."

"Does he play?"

"He did. But he fell and hurt his arm."

"When did he do that? He was fine when I talked to him."

"Not long after that. He slipped on the ice."

"I'm sorry to hear that. Listen, I'd like to stop by and chat with him. When would be a good time?"

"What about this afternoon, Father? George gets home from school around four-thirty. After his science club meeting."

THE TALL, NARROW-FACED Mrs. Madson met me at the front door and led me to a simply furnished living room and down a hallway to George's room. George got up from his computer and greeted me awkwardly, without extending his hand. I turned the desk chair around and sat down, and George sat across from me on the bed. His skin was milky white against his red hair, which had been hidden under the stocking cap the last time I'd seen him. He wore a yellow sweatshirt and blue jeans.

Astronomy posters covered the walls—shots of earth from a satellite, the moon in its various phases, and the terrain of Mars. To break the ice, I asked George about his interest in astronomy. He didn't loosen up. His answers were brief and perfunctory, his blue eyes lowered.

"Your mom says you hurt your arm," I said.

He touched his left elbow. "I fell."

"How did that happen?"

George shrugged. "I was shoveling snow."

I leaned forward, my elbows on my knees. "George, look at me," I said.

He obediently raised his eyes to mine.

"I want to ask you something about Father Edward. Whatever the answer is, I promise, it's all right. So I need you to tell me the absolute truth."

George swallowed. He looked away, as though he considered his response, then he looked me directly in the eye as though he was resolved to speak.

"Did Father Edward make you do anything inappropriate? I mean sexually."

"No!" George blurted, suddenly angry.

"If he did anything, he's to blame. Not you."

"I said no." George folded his arms and stared sullenly at me.

I took this defensiveness as a sign that he was lying. "Please, George," I said reassuringly. "If Father Edward hurt you, it could affect you for the rest of your life unless you get some help to sort it all out."

"I said he didn't touch me," George snapped.

"Did he try?"

George shook his head, resolute.

Now I wondered if he wasn't telling the truth after all, and I was relieved. Maybe the sheer horror at being thought of as queer explained his reluctance. "You didn't like Father Edward," he said. "Did you?"

"He was a priest," George said, as though disliking a man of God was not really an option.

"It doesn't mean you had to like him."

"He didn't do anything to me, Father."

"All right. I believe you. One last question. Did you call me?"

George looked away.

"You did, didn't you? What did you want to talk about?"

George shrugged. "I don't know. I felt guilty."

"About what? George?"

George finally turned back to me. "About calling Father Edward a fag."

"Why did you?" I said, stunned.

"He got on my case for not showing up to do my chores. I got pissed at him." He looked away, ashamed. "I never got the chance to say I was sorry."

DURING A GAME of Ping-Pong, I told Jack about my talk with George. Jack had a cigarette in his mouth, the sleeves of his flannel shirt rolled up, the tail hanging out. We played under fluorescent lights in the west building's large recreation room. He listened quietly as I talked, intent on returning the ball to the very edge of the table on my side. Finally he slammed it to the corner before I could get there to return it, winning the game.

"So, what do you think?" I finally said. "Is George telling the truth?"

With a vague look of disapproval, he lifted his shoulders. "Who knows?" He plopped down on a bench between the Ping-Pong table and the pool table.

I sat down next to him. "You don't think I should have gone to George, do you?"

"You should have known that Eddie wouldn't have hurt him."

I bristled. "Of course, I couldn't believe it. But I had to make sure, didn't I?"

"I mean, Eddie?" he chuckled with a snide sideways glance at me.

His sarcasm puzzled me. Surely he wasn't doubting Eddie's nerve to accost a youth? The confusion must have shown in my eyes, because he eyed me with exasperation, as though I was being dense.

"What?" I said, raising my hands, clueless.

"The magazines you found," he explained. "You *saw* what got Eddie excited. Cops and bikers."

I was relieved. Eddie's wild fantasies were the reason for the snide look I'd seen on Jack's face. "True," I said, grinning.

We played a few more games of Ping-Pong and shut out the lights. As we walked through the corridor past the chapel, I got up the courage to ask if he'd made an appointment with a therapist yet. Three days had passed since he'd made his promise.

"I'll do it," he snapped. "Don't push me."

"It won't get any easier if you put it off. I can ask Alberta for the name of someone."

He scowled at me. "I think you just want me to dump my problems on somebody else so you don't have to deal with them."

The remark astounded me. I stopped and grabbed his arm. "How can you say that? You know I'd be happy to talk about what happened. I can't imagine what it must be like to go through what you did."

"No, you can't. You can't begin to imagine it." He tugged his arm from my grip and continued walking, leaving me standing there, perplexed and hurt.

When I finally caught up with him, he apologized. But he wouldn't continue the discussion, and for the rest of the night he seemed distant.

As I lay awake in bed that night, listening to his steady breathing, I knew that I had set wheels in motion for me and for him and that our future would unfold almost of its own accord. And one thing was certain: nothing would ever be the same for me again, not St. John's, not Jack, not myself. An image came to my mind from a poem I'd read back in our high school days. A falcon trainer stood on a mountain top, his arm protected with a leather gauntlet. The falcon soared around him, making wider and wider circles until the falconer lost sight of the bird. The center gives way, the poem said. "Things fall apart."

Things were falling apart. I couldn't hold them together if I tried.

ON SATURDAY EVENING, I filled in for a vacationing pastor at St. Anne's in Kansas City, hearing confessions and saying the Saturday evening mass. When I returned to St. John's, I drove around the building to see if Jack's light was on yet. His windows were dark. He was still at Santa Rosa's.

Feeling too restless to sit and wait for him, I went to the recreation building, changed into my swimming trunks, and jumped into the pool. I'd finished a dozen laps and was pausing at the edge to adjust my goggles when a hand touched my head. Startled, I looked up to see Danny Flores kneeling over me.

I pushed the goggles up on my forehead. "How did you get in here?" I demanded.

Danny shrugged. "A side door was open."

"No it wasn't."

"Whatever, Father." Danny had a smirk on his face.

I felt vulnerable with him crouching over me, but I was reluctant to climb out and stand practically naked before him. He solved my dilemma by repeating the strip show he'd performed the last time he came to the pool and diving into the water.

I immediately climbed out, determined to throw on my clothes and issue him an ultimatum. Either he left instantly, or I would call the police. As I snatched my towel from the deck, I was surprised to see that the door was shut. Before changing into my trunks in the locker room, I'd propped it open without unlocking the handle so that once I'd finished my laps I could just shut it and not have to bring back the key. Sure enough, when I tried the handle now, it was locked. I padded across the deck to a side door leading to the gym. But it was locked, too. There was no other way out. The translucent fiberglass panels along the outside wall functioned as windows, but they didn't open.

I called to Danny, who now floated on his back in the middle of the pool. My voice reverberated in the enormous room.

Danny raised his head and motioned for me to come join him. Then he laughed.

Furious, I stood with my hands on my hips and stared at him, trying to figure out what to do. Then it occurred to me that if Danny was the one who had broken into the sacristy, he might have found a master key somehow—maybe secretly duplicating Jack's. I picked up his jeans from the deck and searched the pockets, keeping my eyes on Danny, who watched me with curiosity but without alarm. But when I found a key ring and pulled it out, he turned over in the water and began swimming toward me. Hurrying to escape from him, I went to the door, trying one key after the other. I'd gone through four or five keys when he climbed out of the pool, ran across the deck, and wrested the whole set from me. His stunning brown body was dripping, his hair plastered to his head.

"Shame on you, Father. Going through my pockets. I don't have your key."

"Then we're locked in here," I shot back.

Danny grinned mischievously. He backed me against the door, his wet chest heaving from his race across the water. "Locked in together. I like that," he mumbled in a deep, seductive voice. He stroked my arm, pressing closer, his shiny ebony eyes boring into me. Feeling myself drawn into them, I resisted, dropping my gaze. His pectoral muscles formed round mounds, high on his chest, more solid than muscular, like his whole body. His pecs lifted and fell as he caught his breath. Beneath them, the round pat of his belly curved, and his penis, thick as three fingers, began to swell. He pressed it against my thigh as he nosed my ear, his steady breath on my neck.

Becoming aroused despite myself, I halfheartedly tried to shove him away.

"You don't want me, Father?" He chuckled, showering me with his warm breath. "That's not what your dick is saying."

In an instant, he dropped to his haunches, pulled down my trunks and knelt before me, his mouth taking me in hungrily. I sank back against the door, knowing I should resist but immobilized by pleasure.

Suddenly someone pounded on the other side of the door, sending vibrations through my whole body. In the excitement of the moment, I hadn't heard anyone approaching.

"Is someone in there?" The voice belonged to Mike Finney.

Danny glanced up, his dark eyes daring me to answer Mike in this compromised position. How would I explain being locked in with Danny, both of us naked and erect? I remained still until I heard Mike turn around and retreat. Then, involuntarily it seemed, I called out to him.

His footsteps returned. "Father Chris? I don't have the key to the pool with me. It's on a separate ring."

"It's in the pocket of my pants," I called, staring down defiantly at Danny. "They're on a bench in the locker room."

"I'll be right back!"

I pushed Danny away and pulled up my trunks.

"Think I should get dressed?" Danny taunted, falling back and stretching on the concrete floor as though he were modeling for a skin magazine.

"Do it now."

"Yes, Father," Danny said with mock trepidation. He got up and started dressing.

By the time the key turned in the door, I was relieved that my body at least wouldn't betray me.

When Mike stepped in, bundled in a coat, he glanced at Danny and then at me with concern. "Are you all right, Father?" he said.

Danny snorted at the insult. "He was just giving me some spiritual direction, weren't you, Father?"

I glared at him. "This is Danny, Mike. We're both fine. Somehow the door slammed shut. I thought I'd unlocked it."

"Good thing I stopped by," Mike said. "I came to get my cell phone. Left it in my office." He glanced suspiciously at Danny. "Well, if everything's okay, I'll take off."

As he turned, I glanced at Danny, laughing at me with his dark eyes, and called to Mike. "Wait. Would you mind showing Danny out? I'm not sure he can find his way through all the corridors."

Danny threw me a belligerent look. "I can find my way."

"It's no problem," Mike said.

As we walked the short distance between the pool and the lockers, Danny started up about Jack's sermon that night. "Father Jack gave it to them, man. These perverts in the priesthood. Said priests like that should have their balls cut off. Or maybe be killed."

The archbishop had directed his priests to read the Vatican mandate this weekend. Though I'd refused to do it, Jack had probably followed orders. Of course, Danny had embellished Jack's explanation to get at me. I ignored his remark, and so did Mike.

"Where did you park, Danny?" Mike said, curtly.

Danny laughed as though he enjoyed getting a rise out of Mike.

"Thanks, Mike," I said, turning toward the lockers as they continued on.

AT ST. ANNE'S the next day, I knocked over the chalice during mass. It was the first time such an accident had occurred in my fifteen years as a priest. The altar boys stared helplessly as I mopped the wine with the linen napkin used to clean the communion vessels. I nodded toward the cruets on a little table, and one of the boys ran to retrieve more wine.

I'd been jittery since the encounter with Danny. The scene kept playing through my mind—even as I'd slept, it seemed. I would wake up and see Danny's triumphant grin. He had successfully seduced me. I was guilt-ridden, and I was angry for letting myself be manipulated. I was too ashamed to say anything to Jack about the pool incident, and maybe I was afraid that he would accuse me of encouraging Danny or that he'd rashly go after him.

As for Danny, I wasn't sure what to do. Should I turn him in to the police? Get a restraining order? Then I imagined the accusations Danny would make, against me and Jack—complicating our lives even more.

ON THURSDAY MORNING, Debbie buzzed me with a call from David Canston, Jack's older brother, once a seminarian at St. John's, three years ahead of Jack and me. I hadn't spoken to David since he showed up at Jack's graduation with a youthful blond fiancée named Jaime on his arm.

David was a big, lumbering guy, like his father. He was popular at St. John's, a good-looking, easygoing athlete. According to Jack, David had eventually gone into the construction business, having abandoned ideas about ordination when he met Jaime.

I picked up the phone. "David, what a surprise!"

"Hey, man. How's it hanging?" David said in his deep voice, chortling. "So you're the big boss at St. John's now."

"More like the head housekeeper," I said. "What have you been up to? How's Jaime?"

"Shit. We divorced five years ago. Took me for everything. See what you're missing?"

I managed to chuckle.

"Listen." David's tone became serious. "You know what's up with Jack? I haven't heard from him since he moved there. I've been worried. You know, with his history and all."

"He's been busy at Santa Rosa's, I guess. He likes it there."

"So, he hasn't tried to do anything stupid?"

"You mean suicide attempts? No." I thought it was important to name the facts, not to perpetuate shame.

"He scared us all. Jesus, Ben wanted to move into the hospital with him."

"Who?" I thought I'd heard wrong.

"Ben." David laughed. "Hell, he just about came to blows with an orderly. He's got a temper on him."

"Ben's okay?" I was completely confused.

"For a pain in the ass. He's been working for me. He's a good tile man."

"How's the rest of your family? Steve and Pat? Rachel?" Straining to make sense of this unsettling news, I was stabbing in the dark. Maybe Jack, for his own weird reasons, had lied about the name of the sibling who'd come to grief.

"They're okay. Well . . . Rachel just went through a messy divorce. Dad was fit to be tied—a second child with a failed marriage. 'You have to make Christ the third person in your relationship!' " David imitated his father's stern, booming voice.

Distracted by his disturbing revelation, I let him wax on about Mr. Canston's intrusion in his children's marriages. Then I answered mechanically when he finally bothered to ask about my mother, a polite gesture his ex-wife had probably taught him, the Canstons not being particularly interested in anything beyond their own family.

"Look," David said at last, "would you tell my brother to give me a buzz?"

I mumbled that I would. As I started to hang up, I suddenly said, "Why was Jack in the hospital, David?"

"Oh, thought you knew." David sounded uncomfortable.

"I thought I did, too. But I was wrong."

"Man, I can't go into it. I just can't."

"Come on, David. Help me out here."

"You'll have to ask Jack. It's up to him."

After I hung up, I sat back in my chair, stupefied. A voice shouted in my head: *Get away from him. Get the hell away from him.* I felt the inevitability of ending everything, fleeing, cutting my losses. For a while, I may have become immune to Jack's erratic behavior and volatility, but no more. He'd been pretending to go along with me. He was really out of control, a psychopathic liar. How could I ever trust him?

Feeling desperate, I suddenly wondered if I could turn everything around. Keep my mouth shut in the face of the Vatican mandate. Just go on about my business as a simple parish priest, following the rules. Put Jack behind me. Put this whole crazy idea about freedom and a new life behind me.

But as I sat at my desk, the panic eventually subsided. I knew I couldn't change my course. And I wanted some answers about Jack.

I left my office and hurried through the connecting corridor to the central building, running up the stairs and down the corridor to Jack's apartment. I opened Jack's door with my master key. The dark, stuffy living room smelled of stale tobacco. I opened the drapes and started searching through the drawers of Jack's desk. The middle drawer was stuffed with old parish bulletins, holy cards, and sermons scribbled on photocopy paper. The other drawers held prayer books, cigarettes, and jumbled odds and ends. But I found no clues about Jack's hospitalization. I rummaged through the drawer in the nightstand by Jack's bed. Then I searched through the shoes and boxes under the bed and through the contents of the disorderly closet.

The only disturbing thing I found was the revolver, wrapped in a pillowcase and shoved to the back of a shelf high in Jack's closet. I didn't want to think about the gun or that horrible night at the drive-in.

I returned to the living room and began searching the books in the floor-to-ceiling shelves. Noticing that a sheet of folded paper protruded from a thick *Lives of the Saints* on the top shelf, I climbed on a chair and grabbed the book. I sat and opened it to the place where the paper was, unfolding the sheet. It was a page torn from an old St. John's yearbook. In a photo of our sophomore Christmas play, Eddie stood on the stage in a blond wig and strapless blue evening gown. Appropriately, the play was called *That Strange Night.* Eddie had taken the role of Esther, the daughter of a Bethlehem innkeeper who visited the baby Jesus in her father's stable. Our drama teacher, an eccentric nun, got a kick out of making boys play the female roles, often in anachronistic costumes. And Eddie always jumped at the chance.

As I looked at the photo, I vividly remembered Jack making a disapproving remark during a rehearsal of the play, as Eddie sashayed across the stage in the blue gown. Something about Eddie's lack of virility making him a failure as a soldier of Christ. So why had Jack torn out this page? Why had he kept such a photograph?

My eyes fell on the book, which was opened to the story of St. Michael the archangel. In the brilliant color illustration, the muscular figure raised a sword in triumph. A serpent lay crushed beneath his sandal. A chill ran up my spine. I hastily folded the yearbook page, inserted it back into the book, and lifted it to the shelf. But before I could slide the volume back into place, something fell out of the pocket of the plastic cover over the dust jacket. What I saw on the floor shocked me. It was Eddie's rosary ring with the turquoise beads—the ring missing from his finger as he lay in the coffin.

I picked it up and examined it, lying in my palm like a tiny, injured bird that would never fly again.

The room seemed to be closing in on me. I couldn't breathe. I slipped the ring into my pocket. Then I turned out the lights, locked the door, and hurried back to my office.

Jack Canston's Journal

February 16

I read the Vatican mandate from the pulpit. For the first time in my life, I wanted to flip off the Holy Father. Chris is putting this shit in my head. Fight the oppressor, he says. Sounds like treason to me. Sounds like the way to hell. In this life and the next.

But I had another nightmare. This time the Holy Father was with them there, in his white cassock, cape, and skullcap. I screamed to him, but he didn't lift a finger to help.

16

THAT AFTERNOON, AS Jack stood over my desk, grinning at me, my throat tightened and my heart hammered at my ribcage. He'd returned home early and had come to find me in my office where I'd futilely been trying to work all afternoon, despondent about his secrets—the secret that led him to the hospital, and now the incomprehensible secret about Eddie and him. He was the one who'd sent Eddie to despair. He'd come back to the diocese earlier than he'd said and become involved with Eddie. It was their affair that Eddie had confessed to the archbishop. And Eddie had given him his rosary ring.

Jack stepped behind me and kissed me on the head.

My whole body tensed.

"What's wrong?" he said, massaging my shoulders. "You need to relax."

"The door," I said, nodding toward the open door, to make an excuse for my fear.

"Worrywart." Jack shut the door and sat on the sofa. He slipped out the white tab in his clerical shirt and undid the collar button. "I went to my first counseling appointment," he said. "The guy's got me writing down my dreams in a journal."

"That's great," I said, mechanically, feeling that I never had Jack and never would.

Looking puzzled, Jack scrutinized me. "I thought you'd be happy."

"I am."

"He said I could bring you to a session. Since we're a couple." Jack clearly believed the admission would please me.

"Sure. I'll go," I said, unable to muster even a hint of conviction.

"Don't you believe me?" He pulled a business card out of his wallet, got up, and tossed it on the desk. I read the doctor's name, Steven Chalmers.

"It's a private practice," Jack said, perching on the desk.

"How did you find him?"

"My shrink in Montana referred me. Anyway, I've started."

I nodded like a robot.

Jack studied me, disturbed. He reached across the desk and put his hand on mine. "I thought you'd be happy."

I didn't know what to say. I just wanted him to leave.

He got up and moved behind me again. He planted his hands on my shoulders, leaned down, and kissed my cheek. "I love you," he whispered in my ear.

He left the room, still looking puzzled about my reserve, but hesitant to push me. I figured he was fearful that I'd uncovered his past.

As soon as he was gone, I picked up the business card that he had left on my desk and called the therapist's number. A secretary answered.

"This is Jack Canston," I said, not bothering to disguise my voice. I doubted that the secretary would already be able to distinguish between Jack and me. "I was wondering if I left my cell phone in Dr. Chalmers's office."

"The doctor's in session right now, Father Canston. But I'll check afterward. By the way, don't forget to mail back the survey I gave you to fill out."

"Sure." I was relieved, as though confirming this silly fact really made a difference in how I should view Jack. "Oh, here's my cell phone. It was under a stack of papers."

I DIDN'T WANT to sleep in the same bed with Jack that night, but I couldn't think of a convincing excuse, and by then I was praying that somehow I was wrong about him, that sleeping next to him would confirm how ridiculous my suspicions were. But as I watched him get undressed, they only got worse. Love is blind, they say. In that moment I wished I could have been satisfied with blindness, but my love for Jack only seemed to intensify my need to know the awful truth about him and Eddie. It was as though Jack lay wounded in the dark crevice of a canyon, and everything depended on determining his exact position and his exact physical state—no matter how devastating the sight.

Jack climbed into bed. He kissed my throat and stroked my belly. I tensed, but I let him continue. He stripped off my briefs and rolled me onto my stomach. He spread my legs and tongued my crotch and scrotum. I knew what was coming and I was already excited, but then a sense of panic rushed through me as Eddie's chasuble-bedecked corpse flashed before my eyes. When the hard knob of Jack's penis touched my sphincter, the muscle tightened. The more he tried to force himself, the tighter it became.

"Don't you want me?" he said, his chest heaving against my back.

"I'm just not up for it."

I rolled onto my back. Jack lay against me, his head on my chest, until he fell asleep.

As I nodded off, the words from that high school poem drifted through my mind: *things fall apart, things fall apart, things fall apart.*

THE NEXT MORNING in my office, I was still too distracted to work. I couldn't stop thinking about the yearbook photograph of Eddie. I wandered to the auditorium in the northeast building. As I stared at the dark, empty stage, I imagined Eddie under a spotlight in the blond wig, wringing his hands at Mary and Joseph's plight. "Every inn in Bethlehem is full," he declared melodramatically to the bedraggled couple, two of our robed classmates. "I have nowhere to send you."

I remembered the day I'd tried on Eddie's costume without his permission. When he'd found me in the dressing room, he narrowed his eyes, lunged at my throat, and throttled me. The wig flew off my head. He scooped it up and tried to cram the blond tresses into my mouth. I broke loose and ran. He chased me all the way to the chapel, where I claimed sanctuary at the altar. That, he respected, genuflecting to the tabernacle and retreating.

Had Eddie laughed over this story with Jack? Had they been poring over the old yearbook together the first time their hands touched? Is that when Eddie, flashing his boyish blue eyes, had poured on the charm or poured out his heart?

THE COLD DAY was overcast, but Santa Rosa's glowed with a hundred candles. In blue and red glass they flickered like Christmas lights at the side altars, under mosaics of St. Francis, St. Therese, St. Joseph, and St. Rose of Lima. The smell of beeswax sweetened the air. A sprinkling of people knelt throughout the church during the noon mass.

In the vestibule, I stood back from the doorway as Jack lifted the gold chalice at the altar. I imagined the deep disillusionment the people would feel if they knew the truth about him.

After mass, I followed him into the sacristy.

"What are you doing here?" He was beautiful in his Lenten chasuble, deep purple with a Latin American design down the center.

"I'm in town to see Mom. I thought you and I could have lunch."

"This is Tuesday," he said, puzzled. "Don't you see her on Thursdays?"

"We had a lot to talk about."

He nodded, knowingly. "I don't doubt it."

We ate at a Mexican restaurant blocks away from Danny's. Nervous, I prattled about my mother. She'd called me twice since my revelation with hypotheses for why I turned "that way." Maybe it was the Buster Brown clothes she dressed me in. Or maybe she didn't eat right during her pregnancy with me.

Jack listened quietly, reserving judgment, it seemed.

After lunch, when he proposed that we walk over the Branner Bridge, I hesitated. The bridge crossed the Santa Fe railroad yard, which sprawled as far as the eye could see, full of equipment and cable and disassembled railroad cars. The yard abutted a shabby drug-infested neighborhood, on the other side of the bridge.

"Come on," Jack coaxed, buttoning his peacoat. "Let's walk off the burritos."

We trudged up the bridge. When we reached the middle, Jack stopped to light a cigarette. "To-puke-a," he said, gazing at the capitol dome on the downtown skyline. "That's what people in Lawrence it."

"College-town snobs," I said, nervous.

Jack leaned on the concrete banister and exhaled a stream of smoke. "I want to tell you something. The shrink said it's good to talk about it."

I waited, thinking the moment of confession had come.

"It's about the hospital where I stayed. They kept me drugged up. They even did shock therapy."

Stop lying to me, I thought, but I affected concern. "Didn't they stop doing that years ago?"

"It's a new method. It's supposed to reroute the circuits that cause depression. They do it after someone tries to commit suicide. It did seem to help me. I started coming out of my shell. I started playing my guitar again."

I remembered him as a long-haired youth strumming the guitar on his dorm bed and chanting the *Salve Regina,* like a modern troubadour in love with the Virgin Mary.

"This guy at the hospital used to come and listen. Another patient. He had a goofy smile. He reminded me of Ben."

I fought the anger rising in me. I'd see just how far Jack would go. "Why, exactly?" I said.

He shrugged. "His voice. The dopey grin. I don't know. But he told me he'd tried to kill himself, too. Big surprise in that place. He'd been cheating on his wife with a man. Must have seen through me somehow—to confide in me like that. She divorced him. Wouldn't let him see the kids. The judge issued a restraining order."

"Because he was gay?"

Jack chuckled at my indignation. "We're talking rural Montana. The guy was still desperate to see them. I felt sorry for him. He's the first person I ever told about myself."

"Did you sleep with him?" The accusatory remark slipped out of my mouth before I knew it.

"What if I did?" Jack said morosely. He flicked his cigarette over the rail. "I'm trying to tell you how it was. I know things can't work between us if I don't tell you everything."

"Go on."

"That's it. It was a big deal." Jack leaned on his elbows and gazed out at the railroad yard.

"Why were you in the hospital?" I said.

"I told you why."

"The real reason."

He became angry now. "What do you want from me?"

I turned and began walking away. I didn't feel like explaining myself to a pathological liar. Jack suddenly pounced on me, pinning me against the rail.

"Tell me!" he shouted, his eyes wild.

I struggled to get away.

Jack grabbed me by the throat with both hands. I punched him in the stomach.

Grimacing, he released me. It took a second for him to recover. "You don't know what I've been through," he finally said. "You think I can just turn everything off that's happened to me. I'm trying to tell you. Why don't you fucking listen?" He turned and started back down the bridge toward Santa Rosa's.

I rubbed my throat. My heart was thumping in it. I felt confused and desperate. What if I was all wrong about Jack? I'd pay an unbearable price. I would never love anyone again the way I loved Jack.

"Wait!" I shouted. Jogging down to him, I grabbed his arm and turned him around. "I'll listen. I promise."

Strangely wild-eyed once again, Jack grabbed my face and kissed me.

17

THE FOLLOWING AFTERNOON, I drove the archbishop to the airport. He was on his way to a meeting of United States prelates in Washington, DC. Just after I got back to St. John's, the Cursillo group arrived. I showed them to their rooms, ate a sandwich, and went up to feed my fish, watching the sun set out my window.

The rhythmic strumming of guitars echoed through the dark corridor when I went back down the stairs near the main entrance. Then came bad singing. The men and women sounded drunk as they crooned the words to "De Colores," a favorite at local parishes:

De colores, de colores se visten los campos en la primavera . . .
De colores, de colores es el arco iris que vemos salir.

I entered the dark chapel and stationed myself in the confessional. As the group filed past me, still singing, I hummed the English-language version of the song in my head: *Sing of colors, sing of colors that over the hills in profusion are springing . . . Sing of colors, in the rainbow's bright colors God's promise of hope we recall.* On this cold February night, I prayed that the words would come true. That spring would come for me and Jack—new life, resurrection. "Please, God," I whispered, "Please, please, please."

The efficient, dark-eyed Monica Navarro had carefully explained the procedure for the first night of Santa Rosa's Cursillo. The procession from the dormitories to the chapel would end around the altar. There the participants would light candles and fall on their knees in adoration before the sacred host, placed in a golden monstrance by Father Jack. Then, one by one, as the music continued, they would proceed to one of the two confessionals, where Jack and I waited to purify their souls for their mystical encounters with God.

Now the singing ended. Within minutes, the first penitent knelt behind the screen separating our compartments of the confessional. Another followed and then another, and so it went for an hour. A few of the confessions were touching. One man struggled to be a better father. A woman confessed her secret dream of running away from her husband. A teenaged boy fought a drug problem. But most of the confessions were rote, like grocery lists of sins.

After a dozen penitents had come and gone, there was a long silence. I thought I'd offered my last absolution, when the door on the other side opened, and someone knelt behind the screen.

"Bless me, Father, for I have sinned." The soft, bass voice was unmistakable. It belonged to Danny.

"What are you doing here?" I demanded, suddenly unsettled.

"I'm confessing my sins, Padre."

"Not to me," I said. I started to get up.

"I'll follow you," Danny threatened.

I sat back down.

"Aren't you going to ask me when my last confession was?"

I was too pissed to answer.

"All right, I'll tell you anyway. I went to confession to Father Jack a few weeks ago. Since then, I've sinned a lot. I'm ashamed of my sins."

"Just get on with it, Danny!"

"Fuck you, Padre. I'm opening my soul. You're the spiritual guide. It's your job to listen."

I took a deep breath to calm myself. "Go on."

"That's better. I'm not playing. I am ashamed. You were right. I did rip up those vestments."

"Why?"

"I was angry. I offered Father Jack my love, but he didn't love me back."

"He loved you the way he was supposed to. You wanted something else."

"How do you know what I wanted!" Danny's voice rose.

I let him yell. I suddenly didn't care if anyone heard him. He belonged to the Cursillo group. Let them deal with him.

When Danny saw that he didn't get a rise out of me, he seemed to collect himself. His tone became reflective, even sad. "I do the things I would not do. That's how St. Paul describes it, doesn't he? Sin. We do the things we would not do. I want God. Purity. That's what I want. I think the Blessed Virgin loves me no matter what. But I'm not sure about God. Does he love me? Does he forgive me?"

"For what?"

"For all of my sins."

"You know the drill. You name each and every sin. You express genuine remorse. Then I absolve you."

Danny snorted. "You get a kick out of people pouring out their souls to you, Padre? Is it like a power trip?"

"If you don't want absolution . . ."

"No. Wait. Wait." There was a catch in Danny's throat. His voice softened. "I do want to confess. I think you know what. It's like some monster inside of me takes over. I know that sounds like an excuse. But can't Satan possess you? I know the bishop appoints an exorcist. *He* told me that."

"The archbishop?"

"No. Father Jack. He wanted to help me. At first. Then he cut me loose."

"You have to stop stalking us. You have to stop the accusations. You need help, Danny. Professional help."

"It's Satan, Father. He's got me so confused I don't know which way to move. My mind gets twisted. When someone tells you you're an abomination, you don't know whether to kill yourself or kill them. It's a mortal sin either way. But what else can you do, if you can't make yourself something different?"

"What are you saying?" I said, intensely alert now. "Who told you that you're an abomination?"

Danny broke down, sobbing. Finally, he spoke in a halting, broken voice. "When are you supposed to keep a secret and when are you supposed to tell it? Father Jack told me that man's law isn't God's law. So, how do you know?"

As he cried, I puzzled over his secret.

"It's so dark, Father. My soul. It's dark as this fucking confessional. But I can't climb out of it, you know? If I could, if I had balls, I'd cut my way out. Satan's got me anyway. This is useless." Danny started to rise.

"You said the Blessed Virgin helps you," I said, to keep him there. "You know she wouldn't want you to harm yourself. Or anyone else."

Danny settled back on the kneeler.

"Do you know something about Father Gerhardt? Why he committed suicide?"

Danny didn't seem to hear me. "You think she does love me, no matter what? Like a perfect mama?"

"You have to tell me, Danny."

Danny suddenly laughed. "Ask Father Jack. I'll bet he knows. He's the one who's good with secrets. And figuring out what laws you have to obey and what laws you don't."

Confused now, I tried to press him into explaining himself. But it was no use, his guard was up again. He clearly liked having me back in the palm of his hand. I could hear the amusement in his voice as he continued.

"Father, what I want to confess is I screwed a girl last night. She was a virgin. Now she's not pure anymore. It felt good, but I know it was wrong." He rattled off the final formula, "I'm sorry for this and for all the sins of my past life."

I was perplexed and frustrated. Had Danny come to confess his own sin or to torment me with Jack's?

"I'm waiting, Father. I know fornication is a mortal sin. The nuns told us."

At a loss for what to do, I mechanically recited the words of absolution and made the sign of the cross over him.

"Thanks, Father. I feel a lot better."

Not long after he left, a reprisal of "De Colores" swelled up, and slowly the voices faded as the singers marched back to their rooms. I left the confessional. Only the two appointed watchers knelt before the altar, along with Jack, his hands outstretched in cruciform, his eyes closed. Danny was nowhere to be seen.

I silently approached Jack and whispered in his ear. "Come to my apartment, when you're finished."

He nodded without opening his eyes.

I went up to my apartment and paced the living room until Jack finally appeared, looking exhausted. He collapsed on the couch and removed the white tab from his collar. "So, what is it?"

I looked him straight in the face. "I want you to tell me something. Did you have an affair with Eddie?"

Jack let out a strange chuckle and lit a cigarette.

"I found his rosary ring in your book."

He looked surprised. "You went through my stuff?"

"I was looking for the hospital record. You lied to me about Ben. He's not dead. I talked to David."

The expression that came over Jack's face was new to me. It was a kind of desperate shame. But I had no mercy on him.

"Why were you in the hospital?" I said.

He sat quietly without answering. Then he got up and walked out the door.

That's it, I told myself. *You have the answer. Whatever he's done, he doesn't trust you. Let him go.*

But in the next moment, he returned. "Read this," he said, thrusting a spiral notebook at me.

I sat down at the desk with it. Jack moved to the window.

The notebook was apparently a journal. It must have been well hidden, because I didn't come across it in my searches of his apartment. The entry on the open page was dated December 4, only two months ago. The handwriting was bold but sloppy, apparently scribbled in haste. I scanned it, frequently glancing up apprehensively at Jack, unsure of his next move. The recorded thoughts were disjointed, but certain words jumped out at me. *The punks. The fuckers. When I leave here I'll cut their balls off. I'll show them who the fags are.*

"I don't understand this," I finally said. "Who are you talking about here?"

Jack's glance was full of frightening hostility. "They raped me. There were three of them. They dragged me to an alley outside a bar and raped me."

"Gay bashers?" I said, stunned.

"They used a gun. They stuck it up me. A stray dog started barking at them. They killed him instead."

My impulse was to get up and embrace him, but his cold glance said to stay away. "This is why the dog we saw bothered you so much."

"I tried to kill myself," Jack continued, not registering my sympathy, "when my family found out what happened—and the bishop. I wanted to kill myself even if it meant eternity in hell. That's why I got sent to the hospital. I wasn't lying about that."

"Why not tell me? Why the lie about Ben?"

"I tried telling you. I couldn't."

"So you make up this horrible story about your brother? Like I would never find out?"

"I can't explain it," Jack muttered, glancing out the window. "I just couldn't bring myself to say the words."

I scrutinized him. "How do I know you're not lying again? What happened to the men who did it?"

"They never found them."

"Show me the hospital report. The one missing from your file in the archbishop's office."

Jack smiled contemptuously, shaking his head. "You'll just have to believe me."

"No. I want to see the report."

"Go to hell," he said quietly. Then he turned and left the room without shutting the door behind him.

I wanted to stop him. I wanted to grab him and say, *I believe you. I'll never doubt you again.* But the truth was, I didn't know what to believe.

A sickening image of the three rapists flashed through my mind. They were skinheads, grinning at one another, while one shoved the barrel of a gun into Jack. I saw the pain and horror in Jack's brown eyes. Then the dog appeared, a black dog like the one we'd found in the road. Maybe the animal defended Jack because he had petted him on the way to the bar. I saw the dog barking bravely and flying back with the impact of the bullet. Then the punks fled. Jack and the dog remained on the ground, bleeding.

Had Jack been conscious? Had he been able to stand, pull up his pants, and hobble away? Or had someone found him and called an ambulance?

Are you telling me the truth, Jack? Did this happen?

I picked up the phone and called long-distance directory assistance. The operator found a number for David Canston in Butte. It was late, but I punched in the number anyway. It rang three times before David's recording played. I hung up without leaving a message.

I went down to the dark chapel. As I expected, Jack knelt there, his arms once again stretched out, as though he were crucified. Two kneeling women kept vigil next to him, like angelic acolytes.

I got my coat and left the building. The night was clear and cold, a full moon hovering above the bare trees. I trudged across the fields and walked along the split-rail fence separating the St. John's property from the wide, empty pasture.

Questions pounded like a drum in my head. How had Jack's bishop responded to the rape—if it really did happen? Had he grilled Jack about his trip to a gay bar? Did Jack frequent bars? How had Jack tried to kill himself? Had he really used pills? Or had he been lying about that? Had he used a gun—like the one used to torture him? Like the one he had used to threaten the punks at the drive-in?

Struggling for clarity, I kept walking until I reached the road, going all the way to the highway. Instead of crossing it, I turned and walked along its shoulder. I must have marched an hour in the freezing cold.

Then, all at once, the remark of Jack's brother David came back to me. The remark he'd made in our phone conversation all those weeks ago. *You'll have to ask him.* At the time, I'd thought he was concerned about confidentiality. I'd thought he sounded wary. But now it occurred to me that David hadn't been uneasy about betraying Jack's trust. His tone hadn't been one of reserve. It had been one of shame. Realizing that suddenly told me everything I needed to know. Jack wasn't lying about the rape. The shame of it—the shame before David and his whole family—drove him to a suicide attempt.

I had to go to Jack and tell him that I was sorry I'd doubted him, that I understood his lie.

I turned back and ran along the highway. Drivers in the cars that passed me must have thought I was deranged. One driver hit the brights and laid on the horn, but I wasn't fazed. I kept running, and I didn't stop until I'd crossed the fields around St. John's and stood before the entrance, doubled over, my hands on my knees, trying to catch my breath.

I entered the building and went to Jack's apartment. Without knocking, I opened the door. I turned on a lamp in the living room and entered the bedroom where the light faintly reached. I could make out someone in the bed. Then I saw that there were two people, one on top of the other. For a moment I had the startling thought that a couple from the retreat had found their way into Jack's apartment. I felt embarrassed and almost turned around and left the room. But even in the shadows it quickly became clear who was in the bed. Full of rage, I flicked on the overhead light. Danny straddled Jack, who lay with his hands behind his head. They both turned their faces toward me. Jack's face was flushed, his chest still heaving from fucking Danny. Danny smiled with satisfaction.

"Hey, Father Chris. You wanna play, too?" Danny patted his purple erection.

"Get out," Jack said.

"Why?" I said, crushed.

"Just get out."

Danny smirked and began bouncing on Jack.

I left them and returned to my apartment. Picking up Jack's journal from the desk, I flung it across the room. I was gazing helplessly out the window when the living room door opened and Jack walked in. He'd put on his pants, but his chest and feet were bare.

"I was wrong," he said. I could see now that he'd been drinking. His eyes were red and watery.

"Just leave."

"Please, listen to me."

I shook my head. "It's too late."

"I was pissed at you. For calling me a liar."

"I didn't call you a liar."

"The hell you didn't!" he snapped, rubbing his face.

"Get out, Jack. I mean it."

"I'm sorry." He recovered himself. Then he scanned the room, as though searching for the words to make everything right. "Danny told me what happened between you two. At the pool. He said I could ask Mike if I didn't believe him."

I felt the blood rush to my face. "I don't care what Danny said."

"He said he'd go to the archbishop. About you and about us."

"I'll save him the trouble."

That strange, wild-eyed look suddenly came over him. He rushed at me and shoved me against the aquarium. Water slopped over the side. Frightened at himself, he backed away.

"Please, Chris. I'll go crazy without you. I will." He stepped toward me.

I let him draw me into his arms.

As we held each other, Danny appeared at the open door, which I faced. He was still completely naked. He looked defeated when he saw us holding one another. He stared at us without saying a word. I thought he'd just turn around and go away, knowing now how futile it would be to try to take Jack back—even if he truly wanted Jack for himself, not just to torment me. In the initial shock of seeing him standing there, naked, with that sad, untypical look on his face, it took a moment for me to register that he held a gun.

Jack must have felt my body tense. He drew back to look at me and saw me staring in alarm. He must have known Danny was there. As he turned to face him, Danny raised the gun toward us. Jack yelled for him to put it down. But Danny aimed it at me, his eyes now gleaming with malice. Suddenly, Jack lunged at him, and the gun fired. I jumped, then felt relieved. I wasn't hurt. The gun must have fired into the air. Jack tackled Danny, and they struggled on the floor, Jack trying to wrestle the gun away. As their bodies thrashed, I tried to grab the gun, but they rolled to one side before I could. Suddenly the gun fired again. Jack shuddered with the impact. I froze. Then

Jack rolled off Danny. Danny's body was still, his eyes wide open, a bloody hole in his chest.

Jack got up. Panting, and still clutching the gun, he stared at Danny. "Is he dead?"

I knelt down and felt his throat. "Yes."

Jack laid the gun on the desk and sank against it. "It just went off."

"It's your gun, isn't it?" I said.

He nodded.

We stood there, staring at the body.

"He's the one who had an affair with Eddie." My voice was weak.

Jack didn't respond. And I guessed the reason for his reticence.

"He told you in confession. Didn't he?"

Jack remained silent.

"He's dead. There's no reason to keep his confidences. Just tell me the truth. For God's sake, you can go to confession afterwards for breaking the seal!" Exasperated and weak, I got up and collapsed on the couch.

Jack went to my bedroom and brought back the sheet from my bed and covered Danny with it. Then he sat beside me and told me everything. He told me that when Eddie started filling in at Santa Rosa's, Danny had put the moves on him. Eddie succumbed, but he finally repented and cut Danny loose. He told Danny they were both abominations. Jack's voice softened to a whisper. "He gave him the rosary ring. He said he was through with it. Danny gave it to me."

"Eddie thought the ring would bring healing." My were eyes still on Danny.

"It would have! Eddie gave up on it too soon."

I took a breath to steady myself and stood up.

"Where are you going?" Jack said nervously.

"We've gotta call the police."

He nodded, resigned.

While I was on the phone, he left the apartment. At first, I worried that he might do something desperate. But the gun still lay on the desk, where he had put it.

He returned, dressed in clerics now and carrying his satchel. He took out his stole and put it on. Then he knelt and began administering last rites to Danny.

Jack Canston's Journal

February 21

I took a man's life. I fired a gun into his heart. Please, God, tell me he repented for all his sins in the instant before he died. Tell me that in that split second between his heart rupturing and his brain flatlining he beheld all eternity and chose mercy and not damnation.

But his soul is in your hands.

And my soul is blameless. At least for this. When I fired the gun, it wasn't because I looked in Danny's face and saw the face of one of the fuckers in the alley. What I saw was the face of a maniac ready to kill us. Ready to kill Chris. I've never loved anyone like I love him. I'd give my own life for him.

But would I give up what you've given me?

Would I give up my consecration?

18

I ADJUSTED MY new tie in the mirror, smiling at the abstract, squiggly pattern. When was the last time I'd worn a tie to a formal affair and not a Roman collar? I couldn't remember. At the department store, overwhelmed by the huge selection of neckwear, I'd almost gone for safe and traditional. Then, on a brave impulse, I'd picked this one. Afterward, I'd gotten my hair cut shorter than ever. It looked good.

It was almost May now. Over two months had passed since that horrible night in my apartment, which I hadn't slept in since, having moved immediately afterward to an apartment on the other side of the chapel. Now my plans were all made. So were all my decisions. Except for one.

After that awful night, Jack and I had agreed to spend time apart, to think things through, no strings attached. Jack had moved into Corey's rectory, until the one at Santa Rosa's was finished. The contractor in charge of the project had gone bankrupt, and the work had come to a standstill until a new contractor could take over. Since Corey was back on the wagon, the archbishop figured that Jack's company could help him stay sober. Of course, I suspected that Koch just wanted to keep Jack and me apart, which is exactly what we needed anyway.

Maybe Jack did help Corey. I'd never seen Corey in better spirits. He'd agreed to go with me to Mark and Barry's wedding in Lawrence, the reason for my tie. I knew he wanted to probe me about what I planned to say to Jack the next day, my last day at St. John's. But I'd tell him that I didn't know. And I didn't. Not completely. After all, I wasn't sure what Jack would have to say.

It was a balmy Sunday afternoon, and I drove to Lawrence with my window down and my short hair blowing. Along the interstate, light-green feathery foliage waved in the breeze. The sky was watercolor blue. As I exited the turnpike and cut through an old neighborhood of big, gabled houses, I breathed in the clean smell of mown grass.

I found the church on Lawrence's quaint town square. The clapboard building was a little New England–style structure with a single steeple. On the sidewalk in front of it, Corey stood waiting. The curb was lined with parked cars. Since there was no place to park in front of the church, I tapped the horn at him, found a spot down the street, and walked back.

"Thought you'd lost your nerve," Corey teased. He looked good in his sobriety. His freckled face glowed. His blue eyes, so often rheumy and bloodshot, were clear and bright. He wore a white linen jacket and a tie with a tartan pattern.

"What do I have to worry about?" I said, patting his arm. "I'll be a free man tomorrow. I can be as gay as I want."

Corey scowled in mock anger. "And don't you think I'm jealous?"

I knew he was half serious. He was put off that the archbishop had curtailed his membership in gay organizations but appreciative of Koch's extraordinary kindness during his brief return to rehab after the Vatican's mandate had turned him back to the bottle.

We climbed the steps of the stone portico and entered the church to the sound of a festive organ prelude. The organ pipes rose to a central peak in a loft above the pulpit. The white pews on both sides of the aisle were already crowded. We sat in the back pew, climbing over two women with close-cropped hair.

The congregation stood when the organ launched into a trumpet voluntary, and from a door in front the minister emerged in a black robe and white stole. It was the first time in my life I had seen a woman preside at a wedding. She was statuesque, with classic features and salt-and-pepper hair.

Mark and Barry, both in tuxes, walked down the aisle hand in hand. Cameras flashed. A woman in a pantsuit followed the couple with a video camera. Two matronly women wearing corsages on their pastel dresses stepped out of the front pews and kissed them both in a gesture of giving them away. Next to me, a pockmarked man dabbed his eyes with a handkerchief.

So, this is what sanity looked like, I thought. Happy people dressed up and teary-eyed, like the people in every wedding I'd ever officiated at. A nervous couple bravely risking a shared future. So simple and right. Nothing to warrant a menacing dictum from on high.

Of course, I was thinking wistfully of Jack and me as Mark and Barry exchanged vows. Corey seemed to read my mind. He nudged me with his elbow and winked knowingly.

In the receiving line after the ceremony, tall Barry, more suave than ever in his tux, kissed me on the cheek. "We owe this all to you," he said. "Thanks for your advice. We love this church."

"Hey, don't I get some credit for this?" Corey interrupted.

Barry laughed and embraced him.

"You take care of my friend," Corey playfully admonished him, nodding to me. He was thrilled that Barry and Mark were taking me in. They'd cleared out a bedroom, given me a key to the house, and ordered me to water the plants while they honeymooned in the Bahamas.

Burly Mark heard this and turned to me, beaming over the shoulder of a lanky guy in a bad toupee. As the guest moved on to congratulate Mark's mother, Mark threw his arms around me and gave me a bear hug.

Outside on the portico as I chatted with Corey, I waited for him to ask the inevitable question. But he didn't. Not exactly. As a crowd of women and gay men gathered at the bottom of the steps to catch Barry's bouquet, he turned to me and, nodding toward the little crowd, said, "So, is this what you want?"

"Yes," I answered, without hesitation.

He smiled kindly. "Then it'll happen."

Despite the reassuring words, something about his tone unsettled me. He seemed to be saying that my dreams would come true, whether with Jack or with someone else. Did he know something that I didn't?

THE NEXT DAY, I stood in the midst of an office full of packed boxes. Mike had arranged for movers to cart most of my things to a storage shed the next morning. When I'd finished clearing out my last desk drawer, I took the laughing Jesus down from the wall and carried it to Alberta's sun-filled office. She looked up from her desk when I knocked on the open door. She was dressed for the warm spring day in a short-sleeved white blouse, her hair in cornrows under her veil.

"I've got a present for you." I propped the picture on the filing cabinet.

Alberta beamed. "You sure?"

I laughed. "When have I ever been sure of anything?"

"You don't have to be. That's what faith's all about."

She poured a mug of coffee for both of us from the beaker of her coffeemaker, and we sat in two new rattan chairs.

"They finally closed Danny's case," I said. "It was in the paper today."

"I saw. You were never really worried were you?"

I shrugged. "I don't know. Probably more than Jack was. He never doubted there'd be no problem."

"He saved your life. The DA would never question that."

I nodded in agreement. The account of the facts that Jack and I had given had added up. We had both told the whole sordid truth. And Jack had volunteered the confidential facts about Danny and Eddie. Afterward, he'd formally confessed to me his violation of the sacred seal, and I'd given him absolution.

I didn't know what he'd told the archbishop, who must have been asked to corroborate things we said. Jack never told me what he'd said to Koch. For all I knew, he'd lied to him, the way I had lied about the two of us, and the archbishop had pretended to believe him. Or maybe Jack had promised to change his ways, and the archbishop had shown mercy. The archbishop never interrogated me about the events of that night because I'd announced my departure from the priesthood before he'd had the chance to grill me. After my announcement, he'd had little to do with me.

Alberta and I reflectively sipped our coffee, taking in all that had happened at St. John's over a few brief months.

"You start at HNC next week?" she finally said.

I nodded. "I'm a little nervous. My first real job."

"Administration is administration. It doesn't matter whether you're a priest or not."

Alberta's connections had won me an administrative position at the Hospitality Network of Churches. The nonprofit agency helped homeless families find jobs and coordinated temporary housing in churches of various denominations. The pay was low, but it would help me make ends meet as I worked on a master's degree in social work—the field I'd finally decided on.

"When do you talk to Jack?" Alberta said.

"This morning. Before I take off."

"Are you scared?"

I shrugged. "I hope I'll do the right thing."

Alberta touched my hand reassuringly. "You've thought this through. You've listened to your heart. You'll know what to do."

"Since when have you been a romantic?"

"Hey, I've got no problem with being a romantic," she said, shaking her finger at me. "Once I have all the facts."

"And I guess we have all the facts."

She sighed. "More than we need."

THE ARCHBISHOP HAD scheduled an exit interview for ten. Before the dreaded visit, I stopped by the chapel. I knelt in the bright sunlight, inhaling the scent of mowed grass wafting through the ventilation system. The day reminded me of the days at the end of every school year at St. John's—bursting with the excitement of the coming May Day tournament, of graduation, of summer vacation. Festive banners, created by the seniors for their ceremony, hung in the chapel. Noisy boasting and laughter echoed through the corridors, their huge plate windows letting in the lush and vibrant green of the spring foliage.

But mingling with the boyish exuberance was the boyish, repressed anxiety over final good-byes. I remembered the bittersweet feeling when Jack and I had parted ways all those years ago. I felt a glimmer of it now, but unlike those days, in this moment I had a choice, and for all of the poignancy of the moment, I felt that it belonged to me.

When I knocked on the archbishop's open door, he motioned for me to come in and rose from his desk. "Would you like some coffee?" he said.

"No thanks. I've had my limit today." I settled in a wingback chair, wiping my damp palms on my jeans.

The archbishop poured himself a cup and took a seat in the chair facing me. As always his trousers were creased and smooth, his wing tips shining. He wore his jacket over his clerical shirt, as he always did for official business. The gold chain of his pectoral cross, tucked in the vest pocket of his clerical shirt, glimmered through the lapels.

"We've had our differences, Chris," the archbishop began, "but they're all behind us. I hope you know that I wish you well now and that I do not judge you."

"I know you wish me well. But, I'm not sure you can help judging me for who I am." I'd told him the whole truth about myself. And about Danny. I had told him nothing about Jack, or about Jack and me.

"If I judge you, it's out of love."

I smiled and nodded without conviction.

The archbishop seemed genuinely troubled by my disbelief. "You can be deluded about love, you know."

"Everyone can be. Everyone has been."

He frowned in disapproval but held his tongue. "You've served the archdiocese well, Chris. You've been an excellent pastor and administrator. Your parishioners won't forget you, and neither will I."

I thanked him sincerely.

We finished settling some administrative details about keys and bills and information for the new administrator, a priest I barely knew. When I finally stood to leave, the archbishop also rose.

"Will you allow me to bless you?" he said.

I bowed my head, and he made the sign of the cross over me.

When I left his office, I immediately went to the main entrance. Through the glass doors, I saw Jack's pickup in front of the building. I looked for him in the chapel, but he wasn't there. In my apartment, I found a note that he'd slipped under the door, telling me he was waiting outside the recreation building. I found him there, sitting on the concrete steps, looking out at the green fields. He wore his clerical shirt buttoned to the top with the white tab securely in place, not in his breast pocket, as it usually was. I guessed the Roman collar was to make a point about the decision he'd made. It was a decision I'd expected, and I felt only a twinge of disappointment.

"Let's walk," I said.

We strolled past the handball court and climbed the hill that led to the old cross-country course. The long grass in the neighboring pasture stirred in the warm breeze. The blue sky was brilliant.

"I see you've made *your* decision," I said at last.

Jack lit a cigarette. "I want to go on like we were. The counseling is going fine. My life is coming together again. Can't you leave the priesthood and let me stay?"

I shook my head. "No. I can't."

"If we love each other . . ."

"I can't do it, Jack. I'm through with a double life." I gazed around us, imagining the cross-country fans from the past, cheering from the sidelines of the old course, which we now treaded. I suddenly grabbed Jack's arm, and we both stopped walking. I dug Eddie's rosary ring out of my pocket and placed it in his hand. "For healing," I said.

AT NOON, I climbed into my car, my trunk and backseat loaded with clothes and essentials. As I pulled away from St. John's, I stared up at the slender, modern bell tower, at the white buildings framed by green landscaping and azure sky.

I had thought that when I finally left, the strains of one of the old folk songs from the guitar mass days would go through my head.

I did hear guitars, but the song they played surprised me:

Sing of colors, sing of colors that over the hills in profusion are springing! Many colors that shine from God's face, many colors that tell us God's love to recall!

The bright words banished all wistfulness. They were about the future, not the past.